I don't remember my mom too well. She died when I was four, and Daddy doesn't want to talk about her. He's real sad these days. Part of the reason he doesn't smile anymore is that we don't have much money...and he's worried. He never says anything, but I know it's because of me. Because of the accident and all the operations I need to make my leg better so I can walk properly again. My mom's mother and father are real rich, and they want me to go and live with them. But Daddy says he'll mortgage our ranch right down to the floorboards before he'll let them take me away. Daddy's lawyer says they're trying to prove he's not capable of looking after me. He says if Daddy only had a wife, things might be different. I think it would be neat if Daddy got a new wife. Because then I'd have a mother again....

Sarah

Please address questions and book requests to: Silhouette Reader Service
U.S.: 3010 Walden Ave., P.O. Box 1325, Buffalo, NY 14269
Canadian: P.O. Box 609, Fort Erie, Ont. L2A 5X3

Instant Families

NAOMI HORTON
McCONNELL'S BRIDE

Silhouette Books

Published by Silhouette Books
America's Publisher of Contemporary Romance

SILHOUETTE BOOKS
300 East 42nd St.,
New York, N.Y. 10017

ISBN 0-373-30115-4

McCONNELL'S BRIDE

A Letter from the Author

Dear Reader,

Arranged marriages have always been my favorite romance stories—but until *McConnell's Bride* I'd never written one myself. For some reason, I just couldn't come up with a good idea!

Then I was driving through Eugene, Oregon, at the same time a group of environmentalists was staging a demonstration in front of city hall. It was pretty disorganized and not very effective, but it did tie up traffic for miles on a blazing hot afternoon. Tired and hungry, I sat in my car and grumpily decided that no one had put on a decent demonstration since the sixties! For two cents, I fumed, I'd get out and show them how it was done.

But I didn't. As I sat looking out at the ragtag group of well-intentioned, if inept, protesters, I suddenly had a clear image of a woman who *would* stop the car and get this group organized. My heroine was born. The daughter of sixties radicals, her name was Prairie Skye, and she'd never seen a righteous cause she'd been able to pass up yet. Then I looked into the other lane of backed-up traffic and saw a dusty old pickup truck with a clearly irritated rancher at the wheel, a man who undoubtedly had things on his mind and no time in his life for idealistic, would-be hippies with a world to save. And in that brief moment Chase McConnell took life. And with him, the first line of the book: "The obvious answer is to find yourself a woman."

Skye and Chase took over the book right from the start. It was clearly *their* love story, and I was just along for the ride. I've written other arranged-marriage stories since *McConnell's Bride,* but this one is still my favorite, and I'm delighted that Silhouette has reissued it so you could share it with me. I hope you enjoy it.

Naomi Horton

To Bonnie, Lynn, Maureen and Vanessa—
good writers and good friends all,
who make me laugh and—on those rare days when
I threaten to get a "real" job—
remind me that I am, above all, a writer.

Thanks to the doctors and nurses in Lynn's
"Coffee Bunch" at the Nanaimo General Hospital, who
have spent more than one coffee break coming up with
real-life problems for my imaginary characters.

One

―――

"The obvious answer is to find yourself a woman." Phil Duggan leaned well back in the upholstered leather chair and smiled across the wide oak desk. "That would work."

"That's it?" Chase's voice was harsh. "I come in here for advice and that's the best you can give me—to get a woman?"

Duggan shrugged expensively clad shoulders. "If you were married, there'd be no problem."

"Oh," Chase said with a snort, "I'm not just supposed to *find* a woman, now you want me to marry her." He started pacing again, restless and ill at ease. The room stank of leather and polished wood and money, bringing with it fleeting memories he didn't want. "Did you have someone specific in mind, or don't your services run to actual procurement?"

Duggan's eyes lost some of their congeniality. He pulled his foot off the edge of the desk with a thump and pulled the chair closer to the desk, suddenly all business. "You came in here asking for help, McConnell—I'm trying to give it to you. It's time you had a woman in your life again, anyway. It's been three years since—" He stopped, managing to look almost embarrassed. "You've been alone too long, Chase," he added more gently. "You need a wife. And Sarah needs a mother."

It still hit him, that sick, cold feeling in the pit of his stomach. The disbelief. The helpless rage. He fought to keep his expression blank, knowing by Duggan's reaction that he was failing badly. "When I want your opinion on my personal life, Duggan, I'll damned well ask for it. Until then, I'm paying you for your professional advice on how to keep my daughter."

"You're not paying me anything," Phil said, the flare of red across his cheekbones admission enough that he knew only too well the danger he was in. "There's nothing I can tell you that you don't already know, and I won't take a man's money for nothing."

"I don't want your damned charity." Chase's voice snapped through the room, hot with anger. "You bill me for this time just like you'd bill anyone else who walked in here—I'm not down to taking handouts yet."

"This isn't *charity,* you stupid, stubborn son of a—" He managed, barely, to catch himself, fighting visibly to control his rising temper. "I'm a lawyer, not a magician. If your father-in-law decides to walk in here and take Sarah away from you, there isn't a damned thing you or I or the entire state of Oregon can do to stop him. Yes, you're Sarah's father. Under the law—most people's law—that means something. But it doesn't mean a *thing* to a man like Tup Hewitt. He's got the money, the power and the influence to—"

"I know all about Tup Hewitt." Chase's voice was hoarse. He walked across and sat down heavily, forearms on knees, and began turning his dusty Stetson between his hands. He knew Phil was looking at him, could almost feel the other man's sympathy, and for a moment he felt all the despair and the weariness well up and through him. The ache across his shoulders was like a tangible weight pressing him down and he had to consciously fight it off, wondering how much longer that reserve of inner strength was going to last.

"I'm just about at the end," he finally said, his voice little more than a whisper. He didn't look up, staring instead at the hat, turning, turning. "I've had to let the hired hands go—Tom and Annie are all that's left, and I can't afford to keep them. Tom says they'll stay as long as I need them, but . . ." He shook his head. "They're staying because they've been part of the Rocking M spread for forty years, but I won't let them stay without paying them. And I don't know how much longer I'll . . ." He rubbed at a stain on the brim of the hat with his thumb. "That last operation of Sarah's cleaned me out. And the doctors say she'll need at least two more before she'll be able to walk properly again."

"And the insurance?"

Chase gave a bitter laugh. "After Sarah's second operation they raised the premium to close to a thousand a month."

"Can you cover it?"

Chase lifted his gaze to meet the other man's. "I've got a couple of thousand in the bank, Phil. That's it."

Duggan's oath was pungent. "And the bank?"

"I've mortgaged the Rocking M to the hilt, including this year's calf crop. They own me, Phil. Every breath I draw has the bank's stamp all over it."

Duggan's face creased with sympathy. "Why the hell didn't you tell me this sooner? I could have gotten some people together and we could have—"

"No." The word was clipped and Chase held the other man's gaze coolly. "No charity, Phil. I'll get through this somehow. On my own."

Chase thought that Duggan was going to argue, but he subsided, frowning. "And Sarah?"

"Fine. She's doing fine." He managed a fleeting smile. "That last operation got her back on her feet almost. She's using a cane and she tires out easy, but at least she's out of that wheelchair."

"Chase..." Phil stared at him for a long moment, looking like a man being pushed to say something he'd rather keep to himself. "Have you given any thought to just...talking with Hewitt? He's a hard man, but he's reasonable. I'm sure if you just explained the situation, he'd loan you the—"

"I'll see Tup Hewitt in hell before I ask him for help." Chase lunged to his feet again, anger licking at his gut like flame. "And I'll sell the Rocking M right down to the nails in the walls before I take a nickle of his money."

"For crying out loud, Chase, Joanne's dead! When are the two of you going to realize that? This feud you two had over her is finished! Sarah's the one who matters now, not—"

"Leave it alone." Chase's voice was soft, but there was a current of warning in it that rippled through the room like electricity.

"Damn it, Chase, I'm one of your oldest friends! I was *there,* remember? I was at the funeral when he accused you of murdering her. I was at the ranch six months later fishing you out of a bottle of bourbon when you decided you didn't have any reason to go on."

Chase flushed, all the fight going out of him suddenly. He dropped back into the leather chair again, rubbing his eyes wearily. "Tup Hewitt never forgave me for marrying his only daughter, and when Joanne died in that accident he never forgave me for that, either. And now he's trying to take Sarah away from me." He drew in a deep breath, teeth aching where he had them clenched, his chest tight. "She's all I've got left, Phil," he whispered hoarsely. "If I lose her, I've got nothing left to live for."

Phil swore again, looking as though he wanted to say something but didn't know what or how. He held Chase's gaze, his expression filled with pain and understanding and all the things one man wants to say to another who's his friend and hurting. Then he nodded and looked down at the folder lying open on the desk in front of him. "You're sure you want to go through with this?"

"No." Chase managed a humorless smile. "Selling Mary's Mountain is like cutting off a piece of myself and selling it, but Sarah needs two more operations, at least. And then there's therapy to get the strength back in her legs and medication and checkups."

"You're going to run into a lot more local resistance, you know that, don't you? Feelings are already running pretty high around town and the deal's not even finalized yet. People think—"

"People can go to hell. That land has been in my family for three generations, and I'll sell it whenever and to whoever I damn please." Chase heard the ragged anger in his own voice and struggled to lower it. "I'm backed into a corner about as far as I can go, Phil. It's sell Mary's Mountain to Tri-Mar Resorts or lose Sarah. If Tup Hewitt can prove to the courts that I can't afford to give my own daughter the medical care she needs, he *will* get her away from me—don't make any mistake about that."

"But selling Mary's Mountain..." Phil scrubbed his fingers through his hair so he looked, suddenly, like an exasperated schoolboy instead of the lawyer he was. "It's...well, it's like the end of something, Chase. People around here think of that mountain as theirs almost. Hell, most of us learned to swim up in Big Boulder Creek, and got our first kiss in that little spot down by the lake, and shot our first buck up in the valley. There's not a kid around here who doesn't know every trail by heart, and every Sunday there's always a picnic or two by the lake, and—"

"Do you think I don't know how people feel? Selling that land to outsiders is like treason. But I don't have a choice. And if people can't understand that, then to hell with them."

"Most people know the spot you're in. If they had the money, they'd buy the land themselves just so you wouldn't lose it to strangers."

"And then there are the...what the hell are they calling themselves?"

"The Coalition to Save Mary's Mountain," Phil said with a trace of embarrassment. "They're well-intentioned, Chase. Even if they *are* holding protest marches and picketing city hall."

"There's been a bunch of them out at the ranch all week. They had a protest march along the highway this morning, carrying signs and chanting and stopping traffic to hand out leaflets. They were still there when I left."

"And what was our good Sheriff Roy Ives doing about it?"

"Letting them have their way, as long as they stay fairly orderly and don't get on ranch property or start causing any real trouble. He figures it's better just to let them get it out of their system."

"He's probably right. If he starts arresting people, the media will get hold of it and every activist, environmentalist and troublemaker in three states will be up here trying to make a point. This way, they'll get tired of it and go home, and that'll be the end of it."

"With luck," Chase said wearily, getting to his feet. "And Tup Hewitt?"

Phil shook his head. "There's nothing I can do, Chase. He isn't actually threatening you with anything—he's just saying he's going to ask the courts to assess the situation, and to make sure that Sarah's getting the best care available. I'll talk with Sarah's doctors and get a report together—knowing you've got the money to continue her medical care from the sale of Mary's Mountain is a solid point in your favor. But the truth is, you'd have a better chance of swinging the court to your side if you had a wife. Annie might technically fit the bill as full-time female caregiver, but she's still your housekeeper, not a mother and wife."

"There's been no other woman in my life but Joanne," Chase said quietly. "And there never will be. I can't just go out and hire myself a woman to *pretend* to be married to me for a few weeks. So I'll have to take my chances with the courts."

Phil smiled. "Too bad. It would simplify things if you could."

"You're not advising me to break the law are you, Counselor?" Chase asked dryly. "What's the sentence for pretending to be married and lying to a court official, anyway?"

"You don't want to know." Phil stood up and reached across the desk to grasp Chase's hand firmly. "It'll work out, McConnell. And if you need anything—*anything*—call me."

Can you bring Joanne back? Chase asked him silently. And make Sarah whole and well again, and pay off the bank and help me hang on to what's left of the Rocking M? "I will," he lied. And with that, he put his hat on, settling it firmly over his windblown hair, and turned and walked toward the door.

It was the poorest excuse for a protest demonstration she'd ever seen in her life.

And heaven knows, Skye thought, she'd seen plenty of them. Conceived during Martin Luther King's march in Washington in '63, born in the back of a police cruiser during a civil rights protest in Alabama, dragged from one end of the country to the other as her parents had participated in a decade's-worth of protests and sit-ins and marches and demonstrations... if there was one thing she knew, she thought with a hint of bitter amusement, it was how to mount an effective demonstration.

And although all that was firmly behind her now, she still found herself gazing out the car window at the ragtag group of demonstrators with idle interest. Whatever they were protesting, it obviously had something to do with the ranch. The Rocking M Ranch, the sign on the big arched gate read, the words burned into a slab of timber half a foot thick.

She'd find out what it was about soon enough. They'd brought traffic to a stop on the two-lane highway running in front of the ranch gates with a human chain and were going from vehicle to vehicle now, handing out flyers and talking with anyone willing to listen. But aside from that, nothing seemed to be happening.

There were maybe thirty of them altogether. Most were young and fresh faced and exuberant—probably from the nearby college—although a few were older, gray haired and serious. But there wasn't one of them who seemed to know the first thing about putting on a halfway-decent protest.

It was more like a community picnic. Small groups of people gathered here and there, homemade signs resting on shoulders or simply set aside altogether as they chatted and laughed. Some of them had spread blankets on the mown grass along the sides of the highway and were eating sandwiches and sipping soft drinks, and a handful of kids had collected at one side to play a haphazard game of baseball.

Even the occupants of the two police cruisers that were pulled up in the shade of a huge oak tree seemed to be in a festive mood. Two young deputies were leaning against a fence post, soft drink cans in hand, talking with a couple of pretty girls. And an older man—probably the local sheriff—had his elbow resting on the open window of a muddy pickup truck and was talking with the occupant with the congenial, relaxed air of someone who didn't have anything better to do on a hot, lazy Friday afternoon.

And it was hot. The afternoon sun hung in the sky like beaten brass and the rolling hills on either side of the valley held out all but the occasional puff of sultry air. Skye cut the car engine after a moment so it wouldn't overheat and lifted a handful of damp, tangled hair from her nape. This was ridiculous. What in heaven's name could anybody be protesting out here in the middle of nowhere? There was nothing in any direction but ranch land and distant mountains and trees.

She was tempted, for one rash moment, to round them all up and give them a few pointers just to get things moving. But the whim vanished even as she contemplated it, and she smiled again.

Not a chance. She'd made a solemn promise to herself that she wasn't going to get involved in any more "causes." Not after what had happened last time. It had been bad enough when Robert had broken their engagement over what he'd called her "radical activities," but to do it by fax had been the last straw.

Especially when what she'd been doing hadn't even *been* radical. It wasn't as though the owners of the cement plant hadn't been given plenty of time to get their waste system in line with state regulations.

By the time she'd gotten involved, they'd broken enough laws to put them away for years. And the march on the plant hadn't even taken that much organization—people were already so upset that it had taken her a scant day or two to get the almost two hundred angry residents together. The fact that the cement plant had been a client of Robert's law firm hadn't been *her* fault, after all.

Although Robert hadn't seen it that way. His fax had been brief and to the point—he could not, he'd said, marry a woman who incited housewives and small children to acts of civil disobedience and shouted rude slogans at his clients.

In spite of herself, Skye had to smile. The slogans hadn't been rude really—just pointed. And as for the acts of civil disobedience . . . well, fifteen women chaining themselves to the front gates of a cement plant might be seen by some as civil disobedience, but it did get the message across. Especially when the media got hold of it.

Skye's smile widened. It was amazing how cooperative the plant management had become when the crews from six major television stations had appeared at the front gates.

Which didn't have anything to do with *this* protest, she reminded herself impatiently. An intense young man had shoved a flyer into the open window of her car and she looked at it idly. STOP THE RAPE OF MARY'S MOUNTAIN it demanded in inch-high red letters. Under it, in smaller letters, was an emotional plea to help a group calling itself The Coalition to Save Mary's Mountain in its efforts to stop the sale of what sounded like a piece of heaven itself to something called Tri-Mar Resorts.

The background was a rough but effective sketch of a wilderness mountain being plundered by bulldozers, complete with a doe and her fawn cowering in front of a cement truck and three or four fish flopping around on what looked like a parking lot. To one side, a cigar-smoking man she supposed was a banker was shaking hands with a lanky cowboy with dollar bills spilling from the bulging pockets in his denim jacket and jeans.

Again Skye found herself smiling. A little dramatic, maybe, but undeniably effective. Whoever the cowboy was—owner of the Rocking M, she presumed—he was obviously up against some fairly hostile opposition.

And with reason, she found herself thinking, if the description of what Tri-Mar had planned was even vaguely accurate. An eighteen-hole golf course, tennis courts, a huge resort hotel on the lake, a massive campground and trailer-park complex, ski runs for the winter. From what she could see, the entire valley was going to have its quiet way of life turned upside down. It was just too bad that—

No. This was *none* of her business.

Taking a deep breath, Skye folded the flyer and tossed it onto the passenger seat, glancing at her watch.

"Hey, there he is! That's him! That's him!"

The shout made Skye look around in time to see a battered, dusty pickup truck turn off the highway about three car lengths behind her and head for the ranch gate. It stopped a few feet from the closed gate and the far door opened, and Skye watched in sudden interest as a group of protestors, caught by surprise by the unexpected appearance of their foe, started hurrying across.

And an instant later she found herself watching in even greater interest as an extraordinary length of lean, denim-clad male body unfolded from the truck's depths and stood up.

He'd have been pretty hard to miss, even in a crowd. A head taller than nearly everyone around him, he looked as though he'd just stepped off a cigarette billboard, lean face tanned and just a bit hard-edged, mouth tight, eyes as cold as flint in the shadow of his wide-brimmed hat. He raked the growing crowd with a scathing stare that held all the warmth of glacial ice, then turned and strode toward the gate, moving with the deliberate restraint of a man who is holding on to his temper by sheer force of will.

Someone shouted something and the rancher looked around. Skye felt the back of her neck prickle at the fury in that cold, deliberate gaze as it moved over the handful of people around him. He half turned and she could see his fists clench even from where she was sitting, and in the next breath the sheriff—not half as old or as slow as he'd given the impression of being just a moment earlier—was moving swiftly toward the gate. Behind him, the two deputies dropped their soft drinks and headed after him.

There was going to be trouble.

Even as she thought it, Skye was reaching for the door handle. Whatever was going on here, it was on the verge of blowing wide open—and people were going to get hurt unless someone got things under control.

"Now just take it easy, son," Roy Ives said soothingly, planting a large, firm hand on Chase's shoulder. "Don't do something we're all going to regret later, all right?"

Chase shrugged him off angrily. "Get them the hell off my land."

Ives held his stare, as calm and ummovable as old stone. "They're going, son. You just take a deep breath and back off."

"Damn it, Ives, I want these people off my ranch!"

"Well, now," Ives said gently, "they're not rightly *on* the Rocking M. If I was to get all officiouslike and start arresting people, it would cause trouble you don't want. I told 'em a while ago they had until four o'clock to say what they wanted said. Give 'em another fifteen, twenty minutes and we can all go fishing."

It would have done Chase the world of satisfaction in that moment to have taken a full-armed swing at Ives himself, but he managed to hold himself in check. He was just mad as hell, not crazy. Roy Ives gave the impression—to someone who didn't know him—of being fat and slow and not too bright, but Chase had seen him in action. The man moved like a rattlesnake when he wanted to and had a punch that could fell a mule.

Besides, he had to grudgingly admit that Ives was right. No one—technically—was on Rocking M property. They'd been out here for the better part of the week and in all honesty hadn't done anything beyond aggravate the hell out of him. Causing trouble now didn't make any sense.

Taking a deep breath, he shrugged his shoulders to relax them and took a step or two backward, unclenching his fists.

"All right now," Ives was saying to the people who had crowded in around them. "Let's break it up and go on home. It's getting late, and I want to take my grandson fishing."

There was a chuckle or two, an embarrassed glance at Chase, a few nods, and miraculously, the crowd started to melt away.

"We want to talk to McConnell!" One of the young men who'd first spotted his truck gave Chase a challenging look. "We've been out here all week and he hasn't talked to us yet."

"Yeah! How come McConnell won't talk to us?"

Ives's face lost some of its congeniality. "Now looky here, son," he told the boy in his most benevolent voice. "I've been a patient man all week, letting you picket city hall and wander around out here with your signs and all. But enough's enough. Chase McConnell's got a right to do what he wants with his land, and that's a fact. Now you get your stuff together and get on home."

"Excuse me, Sheriff, but these people have a right to have their concerns heard."

It was her hair that Chase saw first. A gleaming mass of tangled, flame red hair that caught the lowering sun and glowed like heated copper. The rest of her—what there *was* of her—was hidden behind Ives's impressive bulk.

"Now look here, young lady," Ives started, his voice vibrating with warning, "this is—"

"The First Amendment gives these people the right of freedom of assembly," the quiet voice went on calmly. "If they are not on private property—and I gather they are not—then you have no legal right to disperse them. Or to keep them from having their say."

"Right on!" someone called from the crowd behind her. "Hey—she's right. Bobby...Bobby, bring those signs back! They can't tell us to go home." There was a mutter from a handful of people, and suddenly the crowd seemed to shift and swell and coalesce into a single unit again.

Ives's two young deputies looked around them in faint alarm, and Chase, curious, took one step to the side to get a better look at Ives's diminutive opponent.

There wasn't a lot of her. Maybe a hundred pounds soaking wet, and most of that bad temper and hair. Hands on narrow hips, she'd planted herself directly in Ives's path and was staring up at him stubbornly.

"Just who the hell are *you*?"

Ives sounded like a man who could see his long-awaited fishing trip being canceled even as he spoke, and Chase saw at least two of the protestors flinch as the bellow rose through the hot afternoon.

But the woman didn't even blink. "None of these people wants trouble—you already know that, Sheriff Ives. They simply want to talk with Mr. McConnell about his decision to—"

"Now look, little lady," Ives rumbled with deceptive congeniality, "why don't you just—"

Bad move. Chase could see it in her eyes even before Ives did, and to his surprise he found himself fighting a smile. "I think I'll leave you and the 'little lady' to handle this between yourselves," he told Ives. Holding the woman's angry gaze, he touched the brim of his hat, then turned and strode to the gate and pulled the latch free.

He pushed the gate open and turned to walk back to the truck just as the redhead stepped past Ives and walked through the gate and across to where he was standing. Her eyes were the color of cut emeralds, he couldn't help noticing, and at the moment they held about the same warmth and softness.

"I think you owe these people the courtesy of an explanation," she said emphatically. "This issue is important to them or they wouldn't be here, and—"

"Lady, you're on my land. And the only courtesy I'm going to show you is not tossing you out on your pretty little backside."

"Why won't you talk to them, for heaven's sake?"

"Yeah, McConnell—why won't you talk to us at least? We just want to—"

"All they want is a chance to tell you how they feel," the woman said with quiet intensity.

"Lady, would you stay *out* of this?" Ives came trotting over. "I almost had this bunch on their way before you came along and got them all riled up again."

"I didn't get anyone 'riled up,'" she snapped. "I just reminded them—and you—of their rights under the Constitution of the—"

"I *know* what Constitution we're under," Ives bawled.

Ignoring Ives, she looked back at Chase. "These people have a right to know why you're selling this land to Tri-Mar Resorts."

"It's none of their damn business," Chase growled, feeling his temper start to rise again.

"This project is going to have a tremendous impact on the people of this community. They should have a say in it. Even if you held a public meeting where everyone could—"

"Like hell."

"So you're going to line your pockets at your neighbor's expense and—"

"Lady, you're really pushing your luck." Chase took a step toward her, but she held her ground, emerald eyes flashing. "You don't know a damned thing about this, so why don't you—"

"Hey. I know who you are!" One of the protestors stepped past Ives, his eyes alight with discovery. "You're that lady who chained herself to the gates of that cement plant just outside Portland last year! You got the whole place shut down because they were polluting the river and—''

Ives's face darkened. "Are you telling me you're not even from around here?"

"That doesn't have anything to do with it," Skye said heatedly, starting to wish she'd stayed in the car. "I don't have to live here to recognize an injustice when I see it! These people have a right to—''

"Are you some kind of professional protestor?" Ives's voice rose dangerously.

"Of course not! I'm a teacher!"

"Hey, Bobby—over here! Quick—bring the rope!"

Ives swung around, swearing, and Skye groaned inwardly as she saw what the four young men were planning to do.

"Hey, Sheriff!" One of the deputies was staring at the ranch gate with a look of absolute astonishment. "They're tying themselves to the gate! What're we gonna do now?"

"We're going to arrest the whole damn lot of them," Ives bellowed, starting to stride toward them. "That's it, by God!"

"No!" Without even thinking about what she was doing, Skye leaped forward and caught McConnell by the arm. He swung around so abruptly that she recoiled, her heart giving a thump as he glared down at her. "Please—call him off. It's my fault...I'll get them to untie themselves and go home. Just call Ives off."

If her plea surprised him, he didn't show it. He stood there unmoving, his eyes unreadable in the shadow cast by his hat, and she swallowed. "Please, Mr. McConnell. They don't deserve this. They're just kids—they don't even know what they're doing."

"They're plenty old enough to know what they're doing."

"They were going home before I stepped in."

"I'd noticed that." His gaze moved over her face curiously, and there was an oddly speculative look in his eyes suddenly that Skye didn't like at all. "Where are you from?"

It was Skye's turn to stand very still. "Portland. Why?"

"And you're a teacher?"

"Yes."

"What do you teach?"

"English and math. And a little history." She didn't know why she added that. Wished, when she saw a hint of satisfaction in his eyes, that she hadn't. "I don't know what any of this has to—"

"What are you doing down here?"

"I...I'm going to Grant's Pass. To visit an old friend."

"So you're on vacation."

"Yes," she replied cautiously.

"Male?"

"What?"

"Is your friend a man? A boyfriend? Lover?" He asked it as though it were the most normal question in the world.

"N-no."

"What are you doing here?" His shrug took in the ranch.

"Nothing! I didn't even intend to come this way, but there was a detour around all that highway construction, then I decided to look for somewhere to have lunch, and the next thing I knew I was out here and they were stopping traffic and—"

"Married?"

Skye blinked. "I beg your pardon?"

"I asked you if you're married."

"What does that have—" Something in his expression made her swallow the rest of her indignation. "No, I'm not married."

"When do you have to be back in Portland?"

Skye's eyes narrowed. "Look, Mr. McConnell, just what are—"

"When?" His voice was clipped.

For a split second she thought of lying, not even knowing why it seemed so important that he not know, but there was something about those cold gray eyes that made her almost afraid to try. "Four... weeks," she whispered. "I have to be back in four weeks."

He nodded very slowly. And then, without taking his gaze from hers, he called, "Ives, I want you to arrest this woman for trespassing."

Two

"**Y**ou want to do *what?*" Ives's bellow made the window in his office door rattle.

"You heard me. Can we do it?"

Ives squinted at him for a long moment. "You been out in the sun without your hat, son?"

"Yes or no, Ives."

Ives pulled at his lower lip, narrowed eyes shrewd. "If it backfires, we could *both* be looking at the world through bars."

"I can't do it unless you're behind me."

Heaving a huge, noisy sigh, Ives shook his head, looking uncharacteristically gloomy. "I'm probably going to live to regret this, but..." A faintly wicked smile flickered around his mouth. Then, as his eyes met Chase's, the smile vanished abruptly, as though Ives had just remembered who he was. "She's smart, McConnell. Damn smart. And she has a pretty good handle on the law. If she gets hold of some hotshot big-city lawyer who doesn't bluff worth a damn, we could be making little rocks out of big rocks."

"If this doesn't work, I don't care what they do to me," Chase said roughly. "Without Sarah, I don't have a damned thing to live for, anyway. So it's up to you, Ives. You're the one with something to lose."

Ives thought about it for a moment or two, scratching absently at his jowly chin, fingers rasping on a late-day growth of graying whiskers. Then he gave a gargantuan snort and heaved himself to his feet. "Hell, boy, I've been playing poker all my life, and I win a little now and again."

His grin suggested he won a lot more than that, but Chase decided now wasn't the time to pursue it.

"Half the game is bluff, the other half is sheer guts. Let's go see what kind of poker player this little gal is."

"You want me to *what?*" The woman stared at him as though not believing what she'd heard.

Which wasn't surprising, Chase thought with grim amusement. He scarcely believed it himself. "I said, I want you to marry me."

"You—you..." She backed away from him as far as she could get in the small jail cell, her eyes as wide as teacups.

She still looked shaken up from her arrest, and even tinier here in the gray surroundings of concrete and bars than she had outside. And for a split second Chase actually felt sorry for her.

But *just* a split second. He was cornered, and she was his ticket out. He'd worry about the morality of it—the right and wrong of it—later. Right now he had to think about Sarah. "Not legally. I just want you to pretend to be my wife for the next two weeks."

"You're out of your mind." She swallowed, looking around as though for an escape—or a weapon—should he suddenly turn violent.

Chase swore under his breath, knowing he was handling things badly and that all he'd done so far was scare the hell out of her. But how did you explain a living nightmare to a woman you'd never seen before? And, in two weeks, would never see again? "I need a wife. A temporary wife. In two weeks, three at the outside, you'll be in Grant's Pass with your friend and that'll be the end of it."

"The end of it, my—" She drew in a deep breath, the disbelief and fear in her rapidly replaced by a deep and healthy anger. "You're absolutely crazy! I'm going to have you arrested for false arrest, harassment, kidnapping and—"

"False arrest?" Chase smiled coolly. "The charges against you are dead legal, Red. You were inside my property line—about three feet inside, as a matter of fact—when Ives arrested you. And you were the one who was harassing me, as far as I can tell." He let his smile widen. "That was one charge I hadn't even thought of."

She swallowed again, holding his gaze with a defiance he would have found amusing under better circumstances. "You can't do this," she said, her voice filled with false bravado. "I have a right to talk to my attorney. You can't hold me in here without—"

"Honey, I figure Ives can do just about anything he wants." He had a twinge of raw guilt even as he said it, seeing the flicker of fear on her face again. But he ignored it and forced himself to stare her down.

He didn't know where the idea had come from. Duggan's suggestion that he needed a wife had been the trigger, obviously, but the actual *plan* had just popped into his head out at the ranch when he'd been standing arguing with her. And although it *was* crazy, odds were it would work.

"I want to talk with my attorney!" Anger and desperation vied for control of her voice and she hugged herself, starting to look sincerely worried now. And scared.

"Well, now, I'd be mighty glad to oblige," a companionable voice said from behind Chase, "but we seem to be having a little trouble with the phones just now." Roy Ives stepped into the open door of the cell, his smile wide and congenial.

"You're lying."

Ives blinked, looking hurt. "Well, now, miss, I don't think you should go calling a man a liar. Not in his own jail cell, anyway."

"I want to know the charges against me." Her voice was crisp, but Chase could detect a hint of panic in it.

Ives scratched his meaty jowl, looking thoughtful. "Well, we've got trespassing. Inciting to riot. Obstruction of—"

"Inciting to *what?*" Apparently forgetting where she was, she took a step toward Ives in her astonishment. "Are you out of your mind? You can't *possibly* hope to hold me on a flimsy, trumped-up, completely ridic—"

"Harassment," Chase put in.

Ives looked at him in surprise. "Well, that's one I never even thought of! That's good, McConnell. That's real good. Harassment." He repeated the word with relish. "I like that."

"You—you can't do this..." she said faintly.

"Well, now, little lady, I figure you should have thought of that before you came into *my* county, getting people all upset." Ives had lost some of his joviality. "This is a real quiet community, miss. We have our problems now and again, but we like to solve 'em ourselves. And it gets me real upset when outsiders come in and start making trouble.''

''But I wasn't—'' She caught it. Took a deep, calming breath. ''Maybe I did overreact a bit. It's just that...'' She held her hands out, her voice placating now. ''Well, I'd been sitting in my car for nearly half an hour, and I just thought—''

''You thought you'd tell me about people's rights and the law and all,'' Ives said helpfully.

''No! I mean—'' Again she struggled to catch her temper. ''As I said, maybe I went a little overboard. But no harm was done. Mr. McConnell wasn't kept off his property, no damage was done to the gate and everyone went home quite peacefully.''

''I'm not fishin'.''

She looked at Ives, expression uncertain. ''Excuse me?''

''I said, I'm not fishin'.'' He gazed at her benignly. ''I was planning on going fishin' with my grandson this afternoon. He's eight—just the age when going fishin' with your grandpa is something kind of important. But I'm *not* fishin', as you can see for yourself. I'm in here, instead.'' His eyes glittered. ''Writing up charges. Taking fingerprints. Doing paperwork.''

She may have paled just slightly, Chase thought.

''I . . . see,'' she said.

''No,'' Ives said quite pleasantly, ''I don't think you do. I go fishin' with my grandson nearly every Friday afternoon. It's sort of a little ritual we have, the boy and me. His dad isn't around—ran off a couple of years back with a waitress from down at the Thunderhead Café. So I take the boy fishin' every Friday and then we go for a hamburger and maybe a movie. Gives my daughter a chance to have some time to herself. I figure that's important to a single mother." He looked at her with interest. "You got kids, miss?"

"No." The one word was a little hoarse.

Ives nodded. "Well, what I'm getting at here, see, is that I don't figure I'm going to have much trouble getting these here charges to stick. Plus any more of 'em that come to mind between now and when Judge Crestwell hears your case."

"And that will be?" She seemed to brace herself.

"Well..." Ives shrugged beefy shoulders. "Could be a while. Henry Crestwell and me—well, we're fishin' buddies. If you catch my meaning."

"All too well." She had definitely paled. But she stood there looking Ives straight in the eye, refusing to back down an inch. Which was either a very good sign, Chase thought. Or a very bad one.

"So what you are basically telling me is that if I don't cooperate with you—with the two of you—I could be in here for days."

"Weeks even," Ives said happily. "It's amazing the amount of paperwork even one small gal like yourself can cause. And the way stuff gets lost around here, with good help being hard to find and all..." He shook his head sadly at the sorry state of the world.

"You do realize, I presume, that when I finally get out of here, I *will* be filing charges against both of you." She said it in the same agreeable tone of voice that Ives had been using, but there was a glitter in her eyes that would have given most men serious pause for thought.

It didn't seem to faze Ives. "Well, little lady, first you've got to *get* out of here." He smiled as he said it, but it still sounded like a threat from where Chase was standing.

"Things don't move too fast in a small town like this in summer," Ives went on gently. "Things can get tied up in court for weeks sometimes, and over the damnedest little things, too. And a thing like this on a woman's record... especially her being a teacher and all. Well..." He shook his head even more sadly. "Hope you weren't planning on making a *career* or nothing out of it, miss. Seems to me that a woman with a criminal record isn't the likeliest candidate for things like promotions and all."

She'd grown more and more quiet while Ives had been talking and she sat down on the edge of the cot with a thump, looking close to tears. "This... this is blackmail," she whispered.

"Call it... oh, call it a mutually beneficial working arrangement," Ives said with a beatific smile.

"Why?" She gazed up at Chase and Ives, looking trapped and despairing. "Why are you doing this to me?"

"I've known young McConnell here since he was born," Ives said, serious now. "People in this community—well, we help each other, miss. When one of us gets in trouble, the rest of us try to help out as best we can. McConnell here is in a tight spot, and he needs himself a wife—just temporary like. My daughter would have done it, but she's leaving day after tomorrow for Seattle."

This couldn't be happening, Skye told herself with false calm. Things like this didn't happen in real life. Not to normal people. Not in *Oregon,* for heaven's sake! In the back hills of Appalachia maybe, but not in picture-perfect little rural villages thirty miles off the Interstate!

And if they found out about this back in Portland?

She closed her eyes, feeling slightly sick at even the thought of it. What in God's name would her friends say? The school board? They'd thrown a fit when she'd chained herself—along with fourteen others—to the front gate of Prideland Cement, and *that* had been for a cause affecting their own community.

The board had been as unimpressed by her heroics as Robert had been, and after a stern lecture about how their teachers were expected to be good role models and conduct themselves accordingly, they'd made it clear that if it happened again, she'd be looking for a job.

If they discovered she'd spent most of her vacation in jail for inciting what Sheriff Ives was calling a *riot*...

"And if I agree?" Her voice was so hoarse the words were little more than a whisper.

"McConnell here will post bail, just to keep everything legallike," Ives said pleasantly.

"When I don't need you anymore," McConnell added quietly, "I'll drop the charges against you and that'll be the end of it."

"So if I agree, I can leave here." She looked up at Ives. "With...him." She let her gaze rest briefly on Mc-Connell.

"Yep." Ives smiled down at her. "Although if you're thinking about going along with this just long enough to get out of jail, then hightailing it the minute you get free, well..."

The smile widened, and Skye found herself thinking of sharks.

"I wouldn't do that, miss. You'd be jumping bail then. Escaping from custody. I'd have to put out an all-points, and every cop in three states would be on the lookout for you. Some of 'em get real unpleasant when chasing down an escaped felon."

And he'd do it, Skye realized. She could see it in his eyes. They'd have her car impounded by now, which meant that even if she did manage to get hold of another one, Ives would just add car theft to the already impressive tally of charges.

If she didn't run—if she just managed to elude arrest long enough to call Robert—would he even come for her? Or would he just figure she was getting what she deserved for not minding her own business? It was late Friday now...it could take a day or more to find another Portland lawyer willing to come down here and help her. And the local ones...Ives probably went fishing with *them,* too!

"You'll never get away with this," she whispered thinly. Knowing they already had.

And it was her own fault. If she'd stuck to her resolve not to get involved in any more "causes"; if she'd stayed in the car; if she'd resisted the temptation to confront McConnell...

If she weren't her parents' child, she thought wearily. It was as though she'd acquired her taste for civil disobedience right in the womb. Or maybe, like red hair and green eyes, it was something you inherited.

"There won't be any...funny stuff. If you're worried about that part of it."

"What?" Slowly she looked up. Discovered that she was alone with McConnell again, and that he was staring down at her with a speculative look on his rugged face. "Funny stuff?"

He looked uncomfortable. "I won't expect the usual... well, intimacies."

"Oh. That's...nice." Skye had a sudden urge to laugh, but fought it down. The man was obviously a lunatic; there was no telling what he might do if she set him off.

"What exactly..." She took a deep breath, deciding to get it over with. "I mean, this is a lot of trouble to go to just to get a wife. Even a temporary one. What is it, exactly, that you need me *for?*"

She thought for a moment that even asking that much was a mistake. The skin tightened around his eyes and he turned away and extended both arms, gripping the bars in his fists. He stood there with his back to her for a long while, arms braced, staring down at the floor.

"I have a seven-year-old daughter," he said finally, his voice rough edged. "She was...hurt. A horse threw her and she—" Skye could see his knuckles whiten around the iron bars.

"She's had to have a lot of medical care—surgery, physio, drugs, rehab. Her—my in-laws figure they can pay for all that easier than I can. They want to take Sarah and raise her." He shoved himself away from the bars and turned to look down at her, his eyes bleak, face ravaged by grief and anger. "They're sending an investigator to check me out. To see if I'm fit to keep her. And my lawyer figures it would be easier to fight them if I—if Sarah had a mother."

It was so far from anything she'd expected that Skye simply stared at him, her mind spinning. It was preposterous...insane...and yet there was something about the pain and the fear and the desperation in his eyes that made it impossible not to believe every word he said.

"I..." She took another deep breath, eased it out again. "Mr. McConnell, I'm sorry. I really am. But you can't possibly expect me to agree to this. It's illegal, for one thing. And there's no way we could convince someone that we're married. I'm a complete stranger. We've never seen each other in our lives before. How could we—"

"They're trying to take my little girl away from me!" He stared at her, his face haggard in the faded sunlight filtering through the window high above them.

It was ridiculous, but for a split second Skye found herself almost agreeing to do it. The pain in his eyes tore at her, and it took more willpower than she'd have imagined to keep from going across to him and offering whatever small comfort she could. "I understand that. But if this investigator finds out you're lying about being married, your in-laws won't need anything more than that to take your daughter from you."

"They won't find out. Ives was right—this is a small community. And a tight one. All the paperwork will be in place. As far as the rest of the world is concerned, you and I *will* be married."

She gazed across the jail cell at him, feeling her heart sink. "You really think you can get away with it, don't you?"

His eyes narrowed slightly, burning into hers. "I'm desperate, lady," he said in a hoarse whisper. "I'll do anything—*anything*—to keep my daughter."

Skye closed her eyes for a moment, fighting panic. He wasn't a lunatic, she told herself firmly. His *scheme* was that of a lunatic, yes, but—desperation aside—the man himself was probably as sane and rational as she. Under better circumstances, he might even be quite nice.

"All I want is two weeks of your time," he said with sudden unexpected softness in his voice. Skye opened her eyes, and found him looking at her with what was almost bleak despair.

"There's a housekeeper, so you won't have to cook or clean or anything. And Sarah won't be any trouble. I . . . look at it as a teaching job, if you want. Sarah missed a lot of her first year of school, and she's behind real bad. I haven't been able to afford a tutor, but when the money comes in from the sale of my land, I'll pay you whatever you think is fair."

And in that moment, the rest of the puzzle fell into place with an almost audible click. She should have seen it, of course. The answer had been there from the moment he'd mentioned the little girl. "That's why you're selling the mountain. To pay for your daughter's medical care."

He didn't say anything. Didn't have to. And suddenly she felt ashamed. "I'm sorry," she whispered, letting her gaze drop from his. "I—I said some things out there. About you wanting to line your pockets at the expense of your neighbors. I'm . . . sorry."

"Save your pity for someone else," McConnell grated. "Are you going to do this, or do I tell Ives to throw the book at you?"

There were probably six-dozen legal loopholes that she could use to be free by nightfall, Skye thought, but at the moment she couldn't see even one. Couldn't see anything, except the weariness on his face, the pain around his eyes. What he was contemplating was kidnapping and black-mail and fraud and heaven knows what else, and yet he was—under it all—no more than a desperate man fighting to keep his family together.

"Do I have a choice?" she whispered after a moment, letting her shoulders slump wearily.

And McConnell, after only the barest pause, just replied, "No."

It didn't take Ives long to get the paperwork done, and Skye realized that getting her agreement had been no more than a formality—they'd both known she had no choice.

There was a moment or two as she stood by Ives's desk that she contemplated tossing common sense out the window and demanding that they just *try* to hold her. That she wanted a lawyer, *now,* and that she was going to make sure that Ives never saw a fishing rod or McConnell his daughter as long as either of them lived.

But in the end it was McConnell's daughter—if, in fact, she even existed—who kept her silent. If he was telling the truth, there was more at stake here than a few broken laws and a quaint, small-town solution to a unique problem. The least she could do was wait to see if there *was* a daughter, and if the in-laws' threat to take her away from McConnell was real. Maybe there was something she could do to help.

Or maybe, she thought with a narrow-eyed look at McConnell, there was another side to this story. What if McConnell really couldn't take care of her, and the grandparents were only trying to protect the girl? In that case, she really should take a closer look at the situation out at the ranch just to make sure the daughter was all right.

Or maybe she should just mind her own business, Skye reminded herself glumly. Except it was too late for that. Refuse to cooperate now, and Ives would throw the book at her—and even if he couldn't make all the charges stick, the resultant uproar would leave her unemployed and persona non grata among her friends.

"Sign here." Ives pointed at the dotted line with a stubby finger. "Full name."

"What am I signing?"

"Just your word that you won't light out for parts unknown the minute you walk out that door," Ives said with the suggestion of amusement in his voice. "You leave Chase here at the altar, so to speak, and I'll be after you like a dog on a rabbit. Agreed?"

"Only because I have no choice," she muttered, signing the paper with a vicious scrawl.

"You got all the choice in the world," Ives said congenially. Then he looked at McConnell. "I'll take care of the paperwork at this end. Far as anyone's concerned, you two are man and wife. You just go on home and take care of business."

Skye turned on one heel and strode across to where McConnell was waiting for her by the door, lounging against the frame as though he had all day. Her suitcase was sitting on the floor beside him, and as she neared, he leaned down and picked it up, then held the door open for her. "After you, sweetheart."

"Don't push it, buster." She stepped by him fastidiously and walked out into the corridor beyond Ives's office. There were four other glass-fronted doors running off it, all closed now, the windows dark, and Skye realized it must be well after six o'clock. "I haven't eaten all day. Are you going to feed me, or am I expected to walk the requisite six paces behind, speak when spoken to and make do with crumbs after all the menfolk are fed?"

"Speaking when spoken to would be nice," McConnell said coolly as he stepped by her. "Any chance of it?"

"Not even one."

"I was afraid of that." A hint of amusement brushed his mouth, gone in an instant. His eyes were shadowed and cool under the wide brim of his hat. "I called the ranch. Annie, my housekeeper, will have a few 'crumbs' waiting for us. Let's get a move on."

He had a long, deliberate stride that Skye found all but impossible to keep up with, and she had to half run to keep from getting left behind as he strode down the corridor and out through the big wooden doors of the courthouse and down the wide steps. By the time they'd reached the sidewalk, she was out of breath and becoming more hostile by the moment.

"What's your name, anyway?" He half turned, waiting for her to catch up. "I forgot to ask Ives."

"What difference does it make? Why don't you just make one up? You're making up everything else."

"You got yourself into this mess, Red," he drawled with infuriating accuracy. "What's your name?"

"Skye."

"I know that. What's the rest of it?"

"There isn't any rest."

He raised an eyebrow.

Skye drew in a deep, calming breath. She always hated this part of it. "Prairie. My full name is Prairie Skye."

"Oh."

She flashed him a heated look. "My parents were into the sixties love-child thing, okay? They didn't want to burden me with a lot of baggage by giving me other people's names. So they gave me an earth name, one that reflects my existence as my own person and...so on." She felt herself flush slightly.

"What do I call you? 'Miss Skye'? Or just 'Prairie'?" He didn't even bother keeping the grin off his face.

Skye look at him for a long, chill moment. "If you're intent on continuing this charade," she said with only a touch of venom, "then I suggest you call me 'darling.'"

The three-quarter of an hour trip back to the ranch seemed to take twice that long. And as the minutes ticked past—each filled with ever-growing hostility emanating from the woman sitting beside him—Chase started to have some serious doubts about the wisdom of what he was doing.

Spending the rest of his life in jail wasn't going to do Sarah any good. And even if he got a lenient judge who wouldn't put him away for about twenty years, the courts sure as hell were not going to view this whole exercise as proof of his competency as a father.

He gave Skye a speculative sidelong glance, wondering what she'd do if he took her back to town and set her loose.

She hadn't said a word from the time she'd stepped into the truck a good half hour ago, and Chase glanced at her again. She was staring straight ahead, chin tipped up, and if it hadn't been for the way her fingers were white where she had her hands clasped in her lap, he'd have almost bought the cool-as-a-cucumber charade.

She was a pretty thing, he had to admit. That tangled mane of fire-engine red hair set off her fair skin and made those wide, dark eyes snap and sparkle. And she was well put together, there was no denying that—it had been damned hard not to notice that she filled out those faded, soft jeans just about perfectly. Or that when she held her shoulders back—as she did now—it only accentuated her small, firm breasts and the slender line of her throat, the spirited tip to her head, the—

Damn it! Chase wrenched his gaze—and disturbingly erotic thoughts—away from the woman seated beside him and concentrated fiercely on the road unwinding in the fading sunlight ahead of them.

Keep your mind on business, he told himself grimly. She's a good-looking woman, but that has no bearing on why she's here. And wouldn't have any bearing in the next two weeks, either. He wasn't looking for a substitute for Joanne, regardless of how empty that big bed got sometimes, and if he let himself get sidetracked, he was going to jeopardize the entire plan.

"What are you going to tell your daughter? About us, I mean?"

It took Chase a moment to realize she'd spoken. He glanced at her and found her looking at him, a frown tucked between her brows. "As far as anyone at the ranch is concerned, we're married. I told Annie I was bringing my wife home. She'll tell Sarah."

"You mean you're going to lie to your own daughter?"

Her voice had risen with disbelief and Chase gave her an impatient look. "The only way we're going to pull this off is if *everyone* believes we're married."

"But..." She looked at him for a long moment. "What happened to Sarah's mother?"

Chase's shoulders stiffened. "What the hell difference does that make? It doesn't have anything to do with this."

"I'm supposed to be your wife. It makes sense that I'd know."

Chase had to fight down the sudden anger, knowing she was right and almost hating her for it. "She's dead," he said thickly.

"Oh." It was just a small, thoughtful sound.

Chase knew she was looking at him but resolutely kept his eyes on the road. Don't ask, he begged her silently. Don't ask the rest of it.

"I'm sorry." She sounded so sincere that Chase glanced at her again. Her gaze met his, filled with an odd gentleness.

"How long has it been?"

"Three . . . years." It was easier than he'd expected for some reason. "It—she was in a car accident." There, he told her. Now you know. Now leave it alone. Leave Joanne out of this.

"Sarah was only four?"

Again the question wasn't the one he'd expected. And again it caught him off-balance. But before he could say anything, she added, "It must be hard, raising a young child like that alone. And running a ranch at the same time, not to mention the concern over Sarah's health. Was she hurt in the same accident that killed your wife? At least I presume she was your wife...."

"She was my wife," Chase said roughly, not looking at her. "And no, Sarah wasn't in the accident. She was home with me when it happened. I already told you she was thrown from a horse." The anger vibrated through the words like heat, and the moment they were out of his mouth Chase was already regretting them. And yet he welcomed them at the same time, welcomed the barricade they provided, the distance it would put between them.

"Yes," she whispered, "you did. I'm sorry."

"Let's get a couple of things straight right now," he said curtly. "We're going to be living together for the next couple of weeks, but we don't have to know any more about each other than we do right now. We're not friends—we're not even acquaintances. I'll tell you what you need to know, but that's it. And my wife and my private life are out of bounds, got that?"

"Yes."

He dared another glance at her, but she was staring out the side window and he couldn't see her face. Not that it mattered what she was thinking, he reminded himself angrily. She'd come into this role with her eyes wide open. If she didn't like the rules, she should learn to stay out of trouble.

"I wasn't asking because I give a damn about you," she said suddenly, her voice soft with anger, "but because you have a seven-year-old child who's already lost one mother. Having me suddenly turn up with no warning and no explanation is going to upset her, and I do *not* want to say something careless that will upset her even more."

He sensed more than saw her turn her head to look at him.

"And I would suggest, Mr. McConnell, that you spend the next two weeks thinking up a plausible excuse for my leaving when the time comes. Because losing her mother when she was four was bad enough. Losing another one three years later could be devastating."

The words went through Chase like a knife. He wrenched the steering wheel to the right, braking hard, and a moment later the truck rocked to a stop on the graveled shoulder. Not bothering to cut the engine, he turned in the seat, anger pulsing through him.

"Get this straight, lady—you're pretending to be my wife for two weeks as part of a business agreement, nothing else. You are not a substitute for my real wife, and you're sure as hell not a substitute mother for my daughter! I'll take care of Sarah. You just speak when spoken to, stay out of my way as much as possible and mind your own damned business when it comes to my family."

Skye recoiled with an indrawn breath of pure outrage. "You—this—I don't need this!" She was reaching for the door handle without even thinking about it. "This whole stupid thing was your idea, McConnell, not mine! I don't even want to be here!" She wrenched the handle and shoved the door wide open. "And if you think I'm going to sit here and take this kind of abuse, you're crazier than I even thought you were!" She was out of the truck in the next breath and started walking hard and fast, too furious even to care where she was going.

"Hey! Hey, where the—"

McConnell's angry bray deteriorated into a growl of irate profanity, and she heard the other truck door open, the sound of running footsteps in gravel behind her. "Keep away from me," she called warningly, not even turning around. "You try and stop me and I'll have you arrested!"

"Lady, you're the one who's already under arrest, remember?"

A hand caught her by the upper arm and swung her half around, and she found herself staring up into McConnell's handsome face.

"Damn it, Red, we're fifty miles from anywhere. Where are you going?"

"I don't care, as long as it gets me away from you! I'd rather spend the next ten years in jail than put up with your—"

"I'm sorry."

"Hostile and completely—"

"I said I'm sorry."

"Irrational..." She ran out of breath and anger at about the same time and found herself glaring up at him, knowing she should be asking—demanding—that he take her to the nearest telephone so she could call Robert. Knowing that she should be raising merry hell at the way she was being treated. Knowing a hundred things, yet able to think of nothing at the moment but the pain in the eyes of the man staring down at her.

She wrenched her arm free, hating herself for even that hint of weakness. "Of course, what can you expect from a man who lies to children!"

"Damn it, I *need* you."

The words sounded torn out of him, as though having to admit that much was almost more than he could bear. His eyes were still as hard as flint, but there was a hint of desperation in them that made it impossible to just turn away.

"Do you think I'd have done this if there was any other way? I'm down to grabbing at straws, lady!"

Skye simply stared up at him, feeling the rest of her anger and outrage drain away. She felt very tired suddenly, wanting nothing more than to curl up under a blanket and sleep until noon, then wake up and find this had all been a bad dream. "I'm just thinking about your daughter, McConnell," she said quietly.

"So am I."

His voice was rough, almost raw, and Skye heard the despair in it. Found herself trying to remember that she didn't care! Everybody had problems. These people and their troubles didn't have anything to do with her. There was nothing she could do. The only thing this silly charade was going to accomplish was to destroy any hope McConnell had of keeping his daughter. It was the act of a madman, and government officials—as she knew only too well—did not like people who made up the rules to suit themselves.

"It's getting late," she finally said, heading back toward the truck. "And you promised to feed me."

The truck was still running, lights on, both doors agape, and Skye wondered what would happen if she just got in and took off with it, leaving Chase McConnell by the side of the road.

She could probably get away with it, too, she mused. By the time he got hold of Ives, she could be clear into the next county, screaming false arrest and demanding an investigation.

Except the uproar that would cause would be almost as bad as the actual arrest itself—the school board, like Sheriff Roy Ives, didn't like troublemakers.

So, in the end, she simply got in and pulled the door closed, and a minute or two later Chase eased himself into the driver's seat. He gave her a look that was half speculation, half amusement.

"Seems to me you just passed up your big chance—keys in the ignition, engine running. Odds are you could have been halfway back to Portland by the time I even found a phone."

"It crossed my mind." She looked at him coolly. "Except I'm in enough trouble now without adding auto theft to the list. I figure Ives probably has fishing buddies in every courtroom in the state."

McConnell smiled, the first real smile she'd seen since she'd met him. It did something intriguing to his eyes, filling them with a compelling male warmth that was distinctly unsettling in a nice kind of way, and Skye's heart gave an unexpected thump in response, making her blink in surprise. In a different place, she found herself thinking a bit dizzily, and at a different time...

"You got that right, honey," he said with a gravelly chuckle. Sweeping off his hat, he raked his fingers through a tangle of dark wavy hair, then resettled it again and tugged the brim down low on his forehead. His eyes were shadowed, and they glittered. "We'll be home in a couple of minutes—try looking a mite more like a blushing bride on her honeymoon, all right?"

Skye's succinct reply just made him laugh.

Three

———

"**So**. This is your new . . . wife."

Annie's expression was anything but welcoming as she let her stare move deliberately from the top of Sky's blazing red head to her small, leather-clad feet. She had set her sturdy frame squarely in the doorway of the sprawling log ranch house, arms folded across her chest, and looked, Chase thought, like a castle guard holding the barbarians at bay until help could arrive.

"That's right." Chase bent down to give her a kiss on the cheek, which earned him a disapproving look but little else. "Skye, this is Annie Lindquist. Her husband, Tom, is my foreman."

"Mrs. Lindquist."

Skye smiled politely, to Chase's relief, and received a chill stare in return.

"Skye." Annie's mouth pursed as though the word had left a bad taste. "Kind of a strange name for a grown woman."

Chase sensed more than actually heard Skye's intake of breath and stepped swiftly between the two women. Whatever female power struggle was going on here would have to wait. "Come on, darling," he said to Skye, dropping his arm around her shoulder. He more or less pulled her past Annie, who—faced with either stepping back or being gently run over—gave way grudgingly.

His endearment got him a frosty smile in return, and a glitter in Skye's green eyes that would have given a weaker man—or a less desperate one—a moment or two of concern. And Chase, smiling right back, decided that this was one power struggle that was going to be dealt with here and now.

Dropping Skye's suitcase on the floor, he pulled her against him firmly, wrapped his other arm around her slender little body, and, with all the zest and enthusiasm of any new groom, dropped his mouth over hers.

He wasn't too certain what to expect as his lips connected with hers—fireworks, probably, and not of the romantic variety. Her lips were cool with night air and extraordinarily soft, and for a split second—before she'd collected her senses enough to react—she filled his arms exactly as a woman should, warm and malleable and eloquently female.

Then, abruptly, she went all unyielding and angular and as sharp edged as a porcupine. She gave a muffled squeak and wrenched her mouth from under his, trying to break free of his embrace. Wrenching her tight against him, he tried to ignore the distinctly unsettling sensations she was causing in the pit of his stomach with as much determination as he was trying to avoid the elbow she was attempting to bury between his ribs.

"Stop it," he growled against her ear, his breath hissing as the elbow connected. "You're my wife, remember?" He emphasized his words by hugging her against him a little more tightly. "Now start acting like it, or I'll take you back to jail."

She went very still, breathing quickly, every muscle in her body as taut as wire, and the outraged fury in her eyes nearly made Chase laugh. "You're bought and half paid for, sister," he reminded her in an undertone. "Now start earning your keep!"

She had freckles, he suddenly realized—not surprisingly, considering her coloring; it was just that he hadn't noticed them before. And her skin was like silk, marred only by the twin spots of red flying high on each cheekbone like medieval war flags. But it was her eyes that intrigued him the most, a dozen shades of green and bronze and six shades of brown, wide and dark lashed and, at the moment, practically smoking with anger.

To her credit—and Chase's relief—she hung on to her obviously threadbare temper and didn't try to gouge his eyes out or plant her knee in his groin, either of which he suspected she'd do at the drop of a hat should the urge hit her. Instead she smiled.

It was a pleasant-enough little smile, and the way she dropped her gaze and then looked up at him from under those thick lashes was enough to make his stomach tighten slightly. But there was something about the too-easy way she'd capitulated that made Chase wary, and it was only when it was too late that he realized she was going to take him at his word.

"All right, darling," she replied in what could only be described as a seductive purr, suddenly all warm, soft curves again as she melted against him. "Let's see if I can't give you your money's worth...."

Her arms were around his neck before he fully realized what she was up to, and in the next instant she'd pulled his head down and was kissing him the way a man only dreams of.

Her lips were warm now and still incredibly soft, but they parted as his mouth dropped on hers, and his heart gave a thump at the seductive, moist touch of her tongue. He should have broken it off right then, but he could no more have torn his mouth from hers and shoved her away in that moment than he could have walked to the moon. Her body was lithe and alive and it moved with delicious and erotic precision against his, touching him in all the right ways, and he tightened his embrace without even thinking about it.

And then he was kissing her back, taking what she was offering with reckless hunger, and after only a moment's hesitation she pressed herself against him with the eagerness of a new young bride. Her tongue swirled and melted against his in a seductive dance that left him light-headed and he could feel his body responding almost violently to the touch and taste of her, raw physical desire surging through him like a tidal bore.

How long, he wondered dazedly...how long had it been since he'd kissed a woman, desired a woman...? How long since he'd even *wanted* to feel that ancient pulsebeat of need coursing through him, had wanted to be aroused, to touch and be touched, to lose himself in the hot, sweet silk of a woman's body...?

Too long, part of him cried out. Oh, Lord, too long....

Only then, somehow, did he realize what he was doing.

And only then, somehow, did he shove her forcefully away from him, breathing hard, aroused and angry and filled with sudden guilt at what he was doing. "Damn you," he breathed, teeth gritted as he glared down at her. "What the hell do you think you're doing?"

For one unprotected heartbeat of time she looked as shaken as he was, her eyes wide and a little glazed, parted lips still moist from his. Then, in an eye-blink, the vulnerability was gone and she was smiling up at him, her multi-hued eyes aglitter with malice.

"Paying my rent, Mr. McConnell. I am your *wife,* remember?"

Wife. The word hit him in the pit of the stomach like a fist, and he swallowed and stepped back, feeling Annie's disapproving stare from right across the big room. What the hell had he been thinking of, anyway, bringing her back here? And why *this* particular charade?

How in God's name had he thought he could pull it off, playing married in this house, where he and Joanne had been so happy. Had—

Sarah.

He used the name as a bulwark against a sudden avalanche of unexpected emotions, ones he hadn't taunted himself with for years. He was doing this for Sarah.

"Don't start enjoying the job too much," he reminded Skye with a cool smile. "You're going to be 'divorced' and back on the road in two weeks."

"Two hours couldn't be soon enough for me," she snapped. "And you were the one who started it!"

Two weeks. How in heaven's name was she going to be able to last two whole weeks?

Skye held McConnell's chilly stare, praying he couldn't see how close she was to losing every shred of control she had left. It served her right, of course, trying to beat a man like McConnell at his own game. She'd wanted to shake him up a bit, to see him lose some of that damned arrogance, and it had worked—to a degree. The problem was, she'd shaken herself up almost as badly.

That hadn't been any pretend kiss, done for Annie Lindquist's benefit. It had been for his own benefit, his own enjoyment, and had been about as real as they come, done with the erotic skill of a man who loved women and sex, and enjoyed both with unapologetic enthusiasm.

Chase McConnell might come across as the original hard-bitten, closed-off lone wolf, but under that flinty exterior dwelled a healthy, red-blooded American male with enough raw sexual energy to light up a small city.

And for the first time since this nightmare had started, she felt a little tremor of apprehension.

"Well, I suppose you're both hungry." Annie strode across and picked up Skye's suitcase. "Dinner's waiting on the table. I guess you want this—" she nodded toward the suitcase "—in the bedroom."

"I can do that," Chase said, moving toward her.

"It's my job," Annie snapped. "You take your *wife* in and feed her. I'll take this in and turn down the bed."

Bed. The one word seemed to reverberate throughout the big living room and settle like a rock in the pit of Skye's stomach. She looked at Chase in faint alarm, but he was striding across to the big stone fireplace that almost filled the entire end wall of the room. *The* bed? Surely to heaven he didn't expect her to—

No. Even Chase McConnell wouldn't carry things to that extreme. In fact, if his reaction to her kiss had been any indication, she wouldn't have to worry about his coming anywhere *near* her during the next couple of weeks.

He seemed to have forgotten she was there. He hunkered down on his heels and started tossing kindling and a crumpled-up ball of newspaper into the fire grate, whistling tunelessly as he lit it.

Not quite knowing what to do, Skye took a step or two toward him, then thought better of it and stayed where she was, looking around curiously. The room was nothing like she'd expected. Somehow she'd envisioned the Rocking M Ranch as a threadbare operation hanging on through sheer guts and desperation, half-buried in debt, with little more than two cows to rub together.

The ranching operation itself might be in financial trouble, but the McConnell clan obviously believed in living in comfort. The big peeled-log ranch house seemed to sprawl lazily in all directions, it and its furnishings built on a large, comfortable scale that seemed suited to big men who worked hard. Men who liked to relax in the evening without worrying about ruining elegant upholstery or perfect floors or knocking over the knickknacks.

The floors were split pine, varnished and well kept but almost proudly showing the wear and tear of passing years. The furniture was all solid and well used, an eclectic collection of colonial and Western and a handful of authentic-looking English antiques that looked oddly at home among the pine and polished oak. Part of the original McConnell family heirlooms?

Skye smiled as she gazed around the room, at the colorful braided rugs scattered here and there, at the groupings of what she supposed were family photographs, some sepiaed with age, others recent snapshots. Oil paintings and woven hangings graced the log walls, and the tables held all the treasured belongings of a family with its roots firmly planted.

What she wouldn't have given to have been raised in a house like this—a *home* like this. Her "home" had been a battered old VW van that had been painted at various times—depending on the state of social unrest at the moment—with slogans and psychedelic flowers and peace signs. Her parents had traveled a lot when she'd been very young, crisscrossing the country as they'd followed the issues of the times.

When she'd been a little older—eight or nine—they'd settled for a while, first in a commune in Haight-Ashbury, where her extended family had numbered anywhere between three and thirty-five and where, for a few confusing months, she'd almost forgotten who her real parents were. Then there had been the farm in Oregon, which in turn had become another commune as people got word and started drifting in and out.

And the whole time, Skye mused, all she'd ever wanted was a real home, a permanent home. A home with ordinary parents with ordinary names living ordinary lives, who would have been quite happy allowing her, too, to be simply ordinary. She looked around the room again, feeling its welcoming warmth enfold her.

No child had ever been named Prairie Skye within these walls—she was certain of that. There had been no political rallies held here, no Zen monks chanting mantras over incense sticks, no pots of "mind-expanding" herbs growing on windowsills . . . nothing but ordinary people living and loving and caring for one another . . .

"You're not going to start crying on me or something, are you?"

Skye glanced around—and up—to find Chase standing there looking at her with a slightly alarmed expression on his face. He'd taken his hat off, and without it, and his thick dark hair tousled like that and the firelight behind him, he looked dangerously handsome and just a little too appealing.

"Crying?"

"You were standing there looking...unhappy."

"Not surprisingly, considering I've been kidnapped." But her heart wasn't really in the repartee, and she shook her head after a moment, smiling faintly. "I was just thinking about something. You have a beautiful home here."

He appeared surprised, and glanced around him as though just seeing things for the first time in a long while. "Yeah. It is. One of the few things I've been able to hang on to."

"People have been happy here, haven't they?" She said it almost absently, hearing the hint of wistfulness in her own voice.

Again he seemed surprised by the question. He looked down at her curiously for a moment, then around at the room again, his features gentling. "Yeah, I guess they have. Funny, I never thought of it that way. It's just always been home. Always been—" He bit the word off and gave her a sharp look, as though suspecting her of being up to something. "Come on," he growled, nodding toward the wide arched doorway leading into the dining room. "You said you were hungry."

Annie had laid out a real ranch-hand's dinner of ham and roast beef and salad and vegetables and a still-warm-from-the-oven cherry pie that Skye suspected—had she been able to eat any—was wonderful. She did manage to swallow a few mouthfuls of ham and baked sweet potato, but she couldn't even taste it, and after a while she stopped even trying.

Chase sat at the end of the table and ate with deliberate concentration, not looking at her, not saying anything, looking more and more foul-tempered as the endless minutes ticked by. Annie came bustling back from wherever she'd been and proceeded to clear away dishes and fuss over Chase. She plied him with coffee and pie and muttered concerns about his well-being, while pointedly ignoring Skye, until finally even Chase had had enough and told her, firmly, to leave them alone and go to bed.

Muttering, Annie ignored him and started clearing away the rest of the dishes. For a rash moment, Skye almost offered to help but she managed to catch herself in time. Her own fear irritated her—Annie's wrath couldn't hurt her, after all. It wasn't as though she was *really* Chase's new bride and was going to have to spend the rest of her life—heaven forbid!—with the woman.

Taking a deep breath, she looked squarely at Annie for the first time since sitting down at the table. "I was hoping to meet Sarah. Is she playing?"

"Playing?" Annie's head shot up and she fixed Skye with a glare that could have cut glass. "At this hour? The child's in bed, of course! She's all worn out, poor little thing. Been on pins and needles all day, waiting for her daddy to bring home his new *wife.*"

The Look, as Skye was starting to think of it, lasered across to where Chase was stirring his coffee. He simply returned it, not saying anything. Then, just as Skye was starting to breathe again, it came whipping back to her.

"I've been taking care of Miss Sarah for three years, *Mrs.* McConnell. Raised six children of my own before that, and all of them turned out just fine. Raised young Chase here, too, and although there are days I wonder where I went wrong, in general he turned out pretty fine, too." There was a pause that could only be called challenging. "How many kids have you got?"

"None whatsoever." Skye felt her cheeks start to get hot and she struggled to hold on to her temper, knowing if it got away from her this time all hell was going to break loose. She had an entire day's worth of frustration, weariness, anger and old-fashioned outrage bottled up, and poor Annie was right in the firing line. "But I am a teacher, Mrs. Lindquist—and a darned good one. I love children and they seem to like me, and I have absolutely no doubt at all that Sarah and I will get along just fine."

The resultant silence almost crackled and Skye was aware of Chase looking at her in surprise. For the barest moment she could have sworn she saw something that might have been grudging approval flicker in Annie's snapping blue eyes, but then it was gone.

Annie drew in a deep breath, as though to launch into a full-blown tirade, but Chase stood up just then. "It's getting late, Annie. Why don't you go on home, and let us clean up the rest of these dishes?"

"Not in my kitchen, you don't." She drew herself up and glared at him. "*I* do all the cleaning up around here, young man, and don't you forget it. You've got troubles enough without—"

"Annie, for crying out loud, this is my wedding night!"

Annie's eyes went wide and a hot blush poured across her features—almost as hot as the one that poured across Skye's. Her mouth tightened and she gathered up a handful of dishes, giving Skye a paralyzing look. "Yes," she said bitterly, "I guess it is at that. You and your new *wife* want to be alone, no doubt. I'll just take these into the kitchen and be on my way." She paused halfway to the kitchen door, the look she gave Chase nearly as frigid as the one she'd given Skye. "And what time would you like breakfast, *Mr.* McConnell? I wouldn't want to come up to the house too early and disturb you."

Chase may have said something under his breath; Skye couldn't be sure.

"That's enough, Annie. Skye is my wife and I want her treated with as much respect as you'd treat any guest in this house."

Annie didn't back down an inch. Straightening her shoulders, she stared him straight in the eye. "But she's not just any guest, is she? She's your *wife*." And with that, she turned on one heel and marched from the room. There was a crash of dishes hitting the counter, and a moment or two later, the bang of a firmly closed door.

Chase did say something then, pungent enough to make Skye wince slightly. He raked his fingers through his hair and turned to gaze down at her. "Look, I'm sorry about that. I knew she was pretty upset, but I didn't think..." He gave his head a shake. "She loved Joanne—my wife—like a daughter. I guess it's hard for her to accept my bringing someone else home."

"I suspect this is only a taste of what you're going to be in for. Are you sure you want to go through with it? If you call it off and let me go, I'll forget it even happened."

He looked tired and drawn and worn right out, and for a moment Skye actually thought he was going to agree with her. But then he smiled very faintly, his eyes implacable. "I told you before, Red—you're my one chance at keeping my daughter. We're going through with it."

It didn't even seem worth the trouble to argue with him, and it was only then that Skye realized just how much the day had taken out of her. Suddenly so tired she could barely stand, she just nodded and got to her feet. "I think you're crazy, but since you're not interested in what I think, I'd like to have a shower and go to bed. If it isn't too much *trouble,* of course."

"No trouble at all." He smiled down at her suddenly, a real smile this time that seemed to ease some of the weariness around his eyes. "You held your own pretty well with

Annie, by the way. You're only the second person I've ever seen who—'' He cut himself off abruptly, the mask coming down over his features again, as cool and remote as stone. "Come on—the bedroom's upstairs."

Skye didn't say anything, simply nodded and followed him thoughtfully across the dining room to the corridor beyond. He'd been talking about Joanne, she thought. The mysterious dead wife whose very name seemed to still cause more pain than loving memories, even three years after her death. You'd think he'd be over the worst of it by now. Three years...a long time to still be hurting so much. To still find it so difficult even to say her name.

It was, she decided as she followed Chase up the long curved staircase to the second floor, going to be a long, *long* two weeks.

As he led Skye into the spacious big bedroom at the end of the corridor, Chase started to wonder if he was going to be able to go through with it. Having her in the house was bad enough; having her in this room . . .

He drew in a deep breath and forced himself to ignore the sudden image he had of Skye lying in bed beside him, that silken skin under his hands, her legs entwined with his. Of what it would be like to make love to her . . . The still-vivid taste of her in his mouth made his gut give a little twist and as impossible as it seemed, he felt his body stir slightly.

Damn it, this wasn't right! Joanne, he told himself almost desperately. He'd loved Joanne. He couldn't feel the same kind of desire, the same kind of wanting, for another woman. Couldn't stand here by the big bed they'd shared and actually contemplate what it would be like to draw this redheaded stranger between the sheets and caress her and lie between her silken thighs and—

He tried to force himself to think of Joanne but found that her image kept eluding him, and for some reason that frightened him almost more than the sudden urge he had to step across to Skye and drop his mouth over hers. To kiss her again, to fill his hands and senses with every sweet, tantalizing inch of her. To take her to bed and—

No!

He caught the fantasy before it could go any further, swearing ferociously under his breath as he strode across and wrenched the window wide open. "Bathroom's through that door. If Annie didn't put towels out, they're in the cupboard by the door."

"I'll manage, thank you." Skye's voice was crisp, but he could hear the exhaustion running through it. She appeared at his elbow suddenly and before he could stop her, she'd reached out and had pulled the window half-closed.

"I don't like *that* much fresh air."

"Well, I do." Just as firmly, he reached out and opened it again. Wide.

Skye looked at him a little uncertainly. "If you're sleeping in here, where am I sleeping?"

"In here."

"But..." The uncertainty was changing, rapidly, to concern as her gaze flickered across to the one big bed. Her eyes widened slightly. "Now wait a minute! Just hold everything, McConnell! This was *not* part of the deal. If you think—"

"Relax, Red," he drawled, moving carefully away from her. Away from the unwanted temptations she provided. "You get the bed—I get the floor. If I was interested in the sex part of this so-called marriage, I'd have hired a professional."

Skye's reply was short and refreshingly earthy, and Chase found himself grinning as he pulled the thick down-filled comforter from the bed and tossed it onto the floor, then followed it with one of the pillows. "I'm going to check the stock, then look in on Sarah," he told her as he walked across to the door. "I'll be back in a half hour or so."

"Fine."

He glanced around at her. "And don't do anything silly like trying to lock me out, Red. A busted door is only going to lead to some interesting speculation about how we spent our wedding night." He didn't wait for her reply.

There was no real need for him to check things—not with Tom still here—but Chase found the ritual strangely comforting. The back corral was full of restless yearling calves and he leaned on the fence and watched them for a few minutes, loving the smells and sounds. They bawled and milled around, the moonlight glinting off an eye or a hoof now and again.

They'd be gone tomorrow, the money they brought no more than a drop in the bucket. But for a few minutes he could tease himself with the way it had been back when the Rocking M had been a big, prosperous operation. There had been a time, and not too long ago, when they'd run a thousand head of prime beef cattle, with the horses and men to handle a herd that big, and the Rocking M brand had been all you could see for a hundred miles in any direction.

The McConnell name had been one to be reckoned with. Bankers smiled at the prospect of dealing with the family, and life had been good. But there had been a few bad years when drought and depressed beef prices and high overhead costs had hurt them. Then his father had made a couple of bad business decisions, stretching himself—and the ranch—too thin. Beef prices had gone even lower, the bankers who had once wooed his business had gotten nervous...

Chase gave his head a shake, scattering the memories. That was all in the past now. His father was dead, and the once-proud Rocking M was mortgaged into the next century. Not really wanting to, he turned and looked west to where the tall, tree-tufted silhouette of Mary's Mountain hugged the sky, black on deep blue.

That mountain had been part of the Rocking M spread since the beginning, when his great-grandfather had first come out to this part of the country to build himself a future. He'd named the mountain after his young wife, and had built the homestead up near Diamond Creek out of logs he'd felled, skinned and notched himself.

The old one-room house was still up there, still standing proud. It was used as a hunting cabin now, although for every year since he'd been about seven, Chase had gone up to spend a few days there himself. It was almost a ritual now, a few days of solitude and introspection, when the past and present seemed very close together.

It was a healing place, too. He'd found himself up there the day after Joanne's funeral, not even remembering the ride up, instinctively seeking the peace and solace he knew he'd find. It hadn't worked, of course, not entirely, but it had gotten him through those first few days when he'd thought he wasn't going to make it. Before he turned to the bottle for those few nightmare months. Before he remembered he still had a daughter to raise...

It would be gone in another few months, he suddenly found himself thinking. The old homestead, the forest behind it. Even the creek was going to be rerouted, according to the blueprints he'd seen in Tri-Mar's proposal. There'd be nothing left, all of it vanished beneath the bulldozer's blade as though it had never existed at all. As though it had never mattered.

A chill wound its way up his back and he swore under his breath, turning away and starting to walk back to the house. They'd understand, all those long-dead Mc-Donnells. They'd faced drought and blizzard, fire and avalanche, flood and storm and even a depression or two. They knew what hard times were, what a man sometimes had to do to survive. Selling Mary's Mountain was the act of a desperate man, but if that's what it took to keep Sarah, he'd sell it twice over.

The house was dark and still when he came back inside. He tossed his jacket over the closest chair and walked through the quiet spaces of his home, checking windows and doors that Annie would have checked hours ago. More ritual. Small things to keep his world in place. He smiled at himself as he stood in the middle of the living room and looked around, seeing it differently tonight for some reason.

People have been happy here. He thought of Skye, of the oddly wistful expression on her face when she'd said it. Funny, how he'd lived here all his life and had never given it much thought beyond the fact that it was home. But people *had* been happy here. McConnells had been born here and had died here, and the years between had been filled with laughter and babies and heartaches and love.

It was pretty quiet these days. No one did much laughing anymore, and Sarah's accident had abruptly stopped the sound of children's happy footsteps.

The door to Sarah's bedroom was open a crack and he nudged it a bit wider and slipped into the moonlit stillness. She was lying on her back, arms and legs asprawl, her small face sweet with sleep. Watching her, Chase felt something pull through him so tight his throat filled with a thick syrupy ache that even swallowing didn't ease.

Her crutches leaned against the wall by the night table, and her new cane, the one she'd been using so proudly this whole past week, was lying on the bed beside her.

He walked across and adjusted the window a bit so the breeze didn't blow right across her. Glancing down at her again, he found her gazing up at him impishly, breaking into a huge smile when their eyes met.

"You thought I was asleep, didn't you?"

"Question is," Chase teased her, squatting beside the bed, "why aren't you? It's late as hell."

This made her giggle, as he'd known it would, and her eyes sparkled in the starlight.

"Is she nice, Daddy?"

"Is who nice?"

She gave an impatient wriggle. "My new mom! Is she nice?"

Damn. Chase had to take a deep breath to ease the tightness in his chest, thinking unwillingly of what Skye had said about a man who lied to children. "Yeah," he said in a rough voice. "Yeah, she's nice." At least it wasn't a complete lie, he reminded himself. For all her argumentativeness, Skye did seem nice enough.

"How come you never told me about her before?"

"Oh, Sarah..." He scrubbed his fingers through his hair. "You sure do ask tough questions sometimes, you know that? I haven't known her for long."

"But you married her." Sarah's wide eyes held his with faint accusation. "How come you never told me you were even going to *get* married?"

"I didn't even tell Annie." It wasn't an answer, he knew.

"But you should have told me," she said softly. "You should have told me, Dad."

"He didn't tell you because he didn't know himself until today, honey." The quiet voice behind Chase startled him slightly. Sarah looked over his shoulder and broke into a wide, shy smile, and Chase looked around to find Skye standing in the doorway.

She walked across to the bed, her eyes meeting Chase's for just a heartbeat—just long enough for him to read the anger in them—and then she looked back at Sarah, her expression gentling. "Your father didn't know I'd agree to marry him until this afternoon. He thought it would be best if he didn't get you and Annie all excited, just in case I broke his heart and said no. Isn't that right . . . darling?"

Skye's gaze met his and Chase just nodded, feeling, in that instant, lower than he'd ever felt before. *A man who lied to children . . .*

Skye sat on the edge of the bed and smiled at Sarah, holding out one slender hand. "I'm Skye. And I'd pretty much bet that you're Sarah."

Sarah shook Skye's hand with the solemnity of a head-office banker. "But Dad never said anything! He didn't even have a girlfriend. Annie's always telling him he *should* have a girlfriend but—"

"Sarah," Chase said with quiet warning, "I don't think Skye wants to hear this."

"Oh, yeah." Sarah's eyes sparkled with mischief. "So I guess you wanted to keep it a secret, huh."

Skye nodded, smiling. Something had changed, Chase thought idly. There was a gentleness in Skye's face and eyes he hadn't seen before, a sweetness almost, and he was finding it increasingly hard to take his eyes off her. She was wearing a long pale yellow robe of some satiny fabric, and he could catch a glimpse of a matching nightgown under it, very short and cut low enough across the top to seriously distract a man.

That incredible mane of fiery red hair—as unmanageable as the woman herself, he suspected—spilled around her shoulders, all waves and curls and flickers of flame. It gave her an ethereal, other-world look, as though if she turned just so he'd see the glimmer of faery-wings in the moonlight or hear the sound of elfin pipes.

"Well, sometimes it's better not to get people's hopes up," Skye said gently, reaching out and brushing a wisp of hair from Sarah's cheek.

It was a natural gesture, done as unconsciously as a mother might, and Chase's heart gave an odd tug, watching her face as she smiled down at Sarah and seeing something there that made him ache with a sudden wanting he didn't even understand.

"Sometimes we do things that hurt other people without meaning to, Sarah," Skye was saying even more gently. "We don't *plan* it that way. In fact, we often do those things because we love the person, because we're trying to do what's best for her."

Sarah nodded solemnly, her eyes locked on Skye's. "I'm glad you're here," she whispered. "I'm glad you and Daddy got married."

Chase gave a choked oath and uncoiled to his feet abruptly, wheeling away from the bed. *What can you expect from a man who lies to children...*

"How did you and Dad meet, anyway?"

He could hear the sheets whisper as Sarah struggled to sit up, could hear the anticipation in her voice.

Skye's laugh was soft.

"Actually, Sarah, that's quite a story—I don't really believe all of it myself yet. But we want to leave something to talk about tomorrow, don't we? Now why don't you snuggle down under here and go back to sleep."

Chase glanced around. Sarah was wriggling her way back under the sheet, her face glowing with excitement and delight.

"Skye sure is a pretty name."

"Well, thank you. So's Sarah...I have a little girl in one of my classes whose name is Sarah."

"Are you a teacher?"

"I sure am. I teach grade four in Portland."

"You don't *look* like a teacher," Sarah said sagely. "Not like the teachers around here, anyway. Are you going to teach at my school?"

Skye hesitated, but just for a moment, smiling as she tugged the sheet and light blanket around Sarah's shoulders. "I haven't made any plans yet, honey. I'm on vacation now."

"No, you're not," Sarah said with a giggle, casting a mischievous look up at Chase. "You're on your honeymoon!"

To Chase's relief, Skye intervened again. Leaning down to kiss Sarah's cheek, she murmured, "Good night. Have sweet dreams."

"Kiss her, Dad." Sarah's eyes sparkled. "You have to kiss her! You're on your honeymoon."

"Sarah..."

"But you have to, Daddy!"

Caught in the lie, Chase leaned down awkwardly, not knowing how Skye was going to react. But to his surprise, she simply put her hand on his shoulders and tipped her mouth up to his as though it were the most natural thing in the world to kiss him. Her lips were soft and slightly parted, and he found himself kissing her more fully than he'd intended, letting his mouth linger on hers for much longer than was either necessary or—by the heat in Skye's eyes—particularly wise.

"'Night," Sarah murmured, her eyes already growing heavy. "I'm really glad you guys got married, even if you didn't let me know before...."

And Chase, kissing his daughter on the cheek, said nothing. He tousled her hair, smiling down at her, then turned and walked from the room.

Skye followed him a couple of minutes later, trying not to slam the door to Chase's—her—bedroom as she closed it behind her. Chase was standing by the window with his broad back to the door, staring out into the night.

"Don't you *ever* expect me to lie to that child again," she said in a furious undertone as she stalked across the room, her bare heels pounding on hardwood. "I covered for you tonight because I couldn't stand the thought of her being hurt, but I won't do it again. Either you tell her the truth, or I will!"

"I didn't ask you to lie to her." Chase turned his head to give her a sullen, angry look. "You walked in there under your own power. I didn't drag you in."

"Oh, that's a clever answer! Am I supposed to stay locked in this room for the next two weeks to avoid having to talk to her?"

Chase's face darkened. He opened his mouth as though to say something, then swore instead and rubbed his eyes wearily, leaning against the window frame. "Look, I—" He swore again, shaking his head. "Forget it, all right? I'll take care of Sarah."

"Break her heart, you mean." Skye turned away and walked toward the bed. "And there are at least two spare bedrooms in this house that I've seen so far, McConnell. If you're not going to take one, I will."

"Like hell," Chase growled. "Four generations of McConnell men have lived in this house, Red, and they all slept *with* their women, not in a spare bed down the hall.

As far as anyone in this house is concerned, you're my wife. And that means you sleep in this bed.''

Skye turned on one heel. "Look, I've had just about enough of your ordering me—'' She stopped dead, her mouth going slightly dry.

He'd pulled his shirt out of his jeans and had unbuttoned it, and she found herself staring without really intending to as he pulled it off and carelessly tossed it across the small armchair in the corner. He was lithe and deeply tanned, with good solid shoulders and muscled forearms that spoke of a lifetime of hard work, and there wasn't an ounce of superfluous fat anywhere on him. A dark swirl of chest hair accentuated the masculine contours of his chest, drew the eye down with almost arrogant deliberation to the flat belly, bared to an almost alarming degree by his low-cut jeans.

Either unaware that she was watching—or simply not giving a damn—he unbuttoned the jeans' waistband, then swiftly drew the zipper down and proceeded to peel them off. He *was* wearing briefs . . . she did notice that much before she finally wrenched her gaze away and spun around so her back was to him, her heart beating crazily.

To her annoyance, her cheeks were burning and she kept her back firmly turned, hoping he hadn't seen her staring at him. She was behaving like an idiot, she told herself ferociously. It wasn't as though she'd never seen a half-naked man before. She'd seen more of Robert that weekend they'd spent at the beach.

Granted, she hadn't shared a bed—or even a bedroom—with him during that time, to his considerable annoyance, but he'd paraded around nine-tenths naked for the entire world to see and she hadn't reacted like this.

Maybe that was it, she found herself thinking a little unsteadily. Robert *had* paraded around, showing off his high-priced tan and his hard-earned physique, both gotten through great expense and diligence at a downtown gym. Chase on the other hand probably never gave his body a second thought unless something hurt, and she doubted he'd been inside a workout gym or tanning booth in his entire life. And there was something healthily erotic about that—and him—that gave her a distinctly odd feeling in the pit of her stomach.

For some reason being suddenly so aware of him made her even more aware of herself—and of the fact that the little nightgown that went with this robe was just that... little. She slipped the robe off finally and shot under the sheet, then curled up on her side with her back to Chase, listening to him moving around as he went through the rituals of bed. Finally the light went out and she could hear him crawling into the folded comforter on the floor beside her, shifting this way and that as he tried to find a comfortable position. Swearing under his breath as he failed. More turning and shifting.

Then he said, "You awake?"

"Not by choice."

"Thanks for being so good with Sarah tonight. She's had a rough three years since her mother died. I never thought... when I decided to bring you here, that part of it never occurred to me, I'll admit that. And I'm glad you... well, that you didn't let how you feel about me affect how you handled the situation in there."

"None of this is her fault." Skye rolled onto her back, easing a deep sigh between her teeth. "McConnell, I hate what you're doing here. Not just because you've ruined my vacation, but because of all the people who could get hurt if something goes wrong. But maybe I can understand it. A little. I... damn." She sat up, frowning, and looked down at him, seeing nothing but his eyes, gleaming faintly in the moonlight. "What I'm trying to say is that although I think the way you're handling it stinks, your motives are . . . honorable. Misguided, but honorable."

His teeth glinted in a smile and she knew he was staring up at her, able to see her more clearly in the moonlight than she could him. "You're a hell of a woman, Red, you know that?"

For some reason she couldn't even begin to fathom, it pleased her. A little flustered, she lay down again, staring up at the ceiling. Then she rolled onto her side, her back to him, and closed her eyes. "Good night, McConnell."

"Yeah," he replied after a while, sounding thoughtful. "Yeah, good night, Skye."

Four

It was a strange damned thing, waking up and finding a woman in his bed. Stranger still, he mused with a faint grin, because he'd been sleeping on the floor....

What little sleeping he'd done, anyway. He'd tossed and turned most of the night, trying not to think about Skye sleeping just a few feet from him. She'd been restless at first and he'd lain there, still and tense, listening to the whisper of cotton sheet on skin, her occasional sleepy sigh.

She talked in her sleep, he knew that. Soft mutters that twice had brought him to his feet, thinking she was speaking to him, before he'd realized she was still sound asleep. He'd stood by the bed looking down at her for a long while, thinking things he had no right thinking. The moonlight had spilled around her and she'd lain against the pale sheets like something out of a dream, tangled hair spread in a pool around her head and shoulders, one hand curled by her cheek.

There had been a moment—just the tiniest flicker of time—when he'd felt a pang of regret that it wasn't Joanne lying there. But it had come and gone so swiftly he'd been aware only of its passing, much more aware of the faint but unmistakable vibration of sexual energy running through him, deep and subtle, like the hum of electricity through high-voltage wires. Or like some machine, he found himself thinking, that had lain silent for years and then suddenly come to life again.

Finally he'd crawled back into his makeshift bed and had lain there, feeling confused and on edge. Finding himself being attracted to her was the *last* damned thing he'd expected to happen. He'd been aware of her as a woman, yes, but only in an abstract sort of way. Or so he'd thought. But maybe, underneath, there had been other motives at work all along....

He'd fallen asleep still thinking about it, his dreams oddly erotic, and had awakened this morning with a curious sense of anticipation. And it was only after he was in the shower, whistling softly to himself as he lathered shampoo into his hair, that he realized with a slight jolt that this was the first morning in three years he'd faced the day with anything but utter despair.

She was still asleep when he got out of the shower, and he found himself making more trips than necessary past the bed as he got dressed, enjoying looking at her. She was lying on her side now, that lake of thick hair glowing like hot copper across the pillow, and he could see the outline of her hip and thigh under the bedcovers, the silken curve of exposed shoulder. It seemed oddly right seeing her there in his bed and he allowed himself a moment or two of idle fantasy, teasing himself with the thought of really being married to her...

And then, realizing what he was doing, he swore softly and strode back into the bathroom, tossing his shirt aside until he'd finished shaving. His image in the mirror gazed back at him slightly accusingly, and he looked away and concentrated instead on guiding the razor down his cheek.

He heard the slow, determined footsteps on the stairs just as he'd finished shaving and he stepped into the bedroom, listening intently. Skye was awake. She was propped up on one elbow, looking sleepy and a little puzzled, as though uncertain of where she was.

The footsteps had reached the top of the stairs, and Chase's eyes narrowed. Absently he wiped shaving foam off his jaw, aware that Skye was watching him. He had his mouth half open to say something to her, when the footsteps turned and started walking down the corridor toward the bedroom, heels rapping smartly on the hardwood.

Swearing ferociously, Chase flung the towel down and catapulted across the room to snatch up the comforter and pillow from the floor. And before Skye could even react, he vaulted across her lightly and slipped under the covers.

"Wedding breakfast in bed," he growled, tearing his jeans off. He pulled them from under the covers and tossed them across the room. "An old McConnell tradition I didn't figure she'd bother with this time around." His words coincided with a sharp rap at the door, and a moment later the knob turned and the door swung inward.

And before Skye could even draw in a breath to protest, he'd pulled her into his arms and was kissing her as though there was no tomorrow.

She went rigid with shock and he tightened his embrace, cradling her head to keep her from wrenching away. After a moment, he drew his lips from hers and turned his head to look at Annie, who was striding across the room to put the tray onto the dresser.

"Damn it to hell, Annie," he drawled. "You shouldn't just come barging into a man's room like this."

"I knocked." She put the tray down with a bang that made the coffee cups rattle. "Besides, I heard the shower. Serving the bride and groom breakfast in bed is a tradition in this house."

To Chase's relief, Skye—catching on more quickly than he could have even hoped—went very still in his arms. He could feel her warm breath curling around his throat and swore he could even sense her heartbeat against his. It was distracting, having his arms full of warm, sweet-scented woman like this, and he had to force himself to concentrate to keep his mind from drifting into a variety of unnecessary directions, none of which had a damned thing to do with convincing Annie that he and Skye were married.

Annie was bustling around the room, picking up his hastily discarded jeans from one corner and his socks from another, muttering as she snatched up Skye's blouse and put it on a padded hanger and tucked it into the closet.

"Annie, can't you do that later?"

"Now's as good a time as any. It's getting late. Time most people were out of bed and hard at work."

Chase swore under his breath, a confrontation with Annie right now the *last* thing he wanted. She'd been the mainstay of this old house for close to forty years, and he needed her support as badly as he needed her to believe that he and Skye were man and wife.

"Cut me a little slack, Annie," he murmured, burying his face against Skye's sweet-scented throat. "I just got married. The Rocking M isn't going to fall apart if I don't get downstairs in the next five minutes."

Skye drew in a sharp little breath as he let his mouth browse lightly up to the downy hollow under her ear. She lay nestled against him as happily—and cooperatively—as any real wife would, even slipping her arm around his shoulder. Warm, with skin like silk, she was more naked than not, a fact he hadn't really considered when he'd dived into bed beside her, and as he drew his mouth across her cheek, his mind started to wander again. Her hair billowed around her face, as soft as spun sugar, and it caught in the work-roughened skin of his hand as he smoothed it back from her face.

He'd slipped his thigh between hers more intimately than he'd intended to, and he was becoming more and more aware of the feel of her bare skin against his, the curved weight of her breast against his arm, the tantalizing fact that there was nothing at all between them but a wispy film of satin that was more erotic for what it promised than what it hid.

Her mouth was under his suddenly, and although he hadn't consciously decided to kiss her again, it seemed like the logical thing to do. Especially with Annie still bustling around in the background, pretending not to notice. As he pressed his lips over hers, teasing them apart with the tip of his tongue, it occurred to him, just fleetingly, that there was probably no need to carry the "pretending" quite this far. That in all likelihood, as a matter of fact, he probably didn't have to even *touch* her lips with his to fake a thoroughly acceptable kiss.

But Skye was responding with satisfying realism herself by then, so there didn't seem to be any need to worry about the propriety of it. No need to worry about anything, in fact, but the sweet taste of her and the things it was doing to his heart rate.

He tightened his fingers in her thick hair involuntarily and found himself suddenly kissing her with more enthusiasm than was technically necessary, letting himself sink into the hot, erotic taste of her as though it really meant something.

Needing . . . oh, God, suddenly needing the touch of a woman, relishing the near pain of sudden and very real desire, wanting to . . .

A door banged with cataclysmic force and Chase decided dimly that Annie had probably left. It occurred to him in a vague and distracted way that there was no need to keep kissing Skye. That he could get back to his shaving with little likelihood of further interruptions. That any minute now Skye would be screaming her head off and demanding he leave her alone.

She did give a soft little whimper in her throat just then, but it seemed to be less protest than encouragement, and instead of disentangling himself from her as he ought to be doing, he turned his head to kiss her even more deeply. A shudder ran through her and she moved in his arms slightly, her body caressing his, and for a moment Chase thought he was going to lose it then and there. And that in the brief moment it took to strip her out of that damned nightgown, three long years of voluntary celibacy were going to be over.

Skye tore her mouth from under his and pressed her face against his shoulder, her heart hammering like a runaway flywheel. "This . . . this *is* . . . just . . . pretend," she whispered brokenly.

Chase realized he had his teeth gritted so hard his jaw ached. He held on to her tightly, eyes squeezed closed as he pressed his cheek against her hair. "Yeah, Red, it's just pretend."

But he didn't want the pretending to end, he found himself thinking desperately. Not yet... please, not yet. It had been half a lifetime since he'd ached with this kind of want and he didn't want to go back to the cold, despairing emptiness again.

He wanted her. Wanted to drown himself in the sweet nectar of her kisses, to run his hand down the long sweep of her back, then back up to cup and caress her naked breasts and feel the nipples tighten with expectation. Wanted to slide between her legs and sink down, down, down into the female warmth she held hidden there and to love her until she was crying out and then bring them both to savage and utter completion and collapse laughing and exhausted into her arms.

And he couldn't, he reminded himself with weary despair. Because this whole damned thing was just a charade that didn't mean anything at all.

Slowly he eased himself away from her. Skye looked dazed, her parted lips swollen, eyes heavy lidded. He could see the pulse in her throat fluttering and found himself wanting to lower his mouth to it.

Instead, he eased himself out of bed without looking at her and padded across to the big chest of drawers to retrieve his jeans, which Annie had meticulously folded and put away.

Something was going on here. Something he didn't understand. He'd spent the last three years in an emotional stasis, too numbed by grief to feel, to think, to want. A robot, almost, programmed to go through the motions of being a man but with every physical and emotional response turned off.

Three years. And never—not one damned time in that whole stretch—had he been even vaguely interested in a woman. Not once. And now, over the span of a day, he was behaving like a stallion scenting his first mare, ready to tear up the ground and scream at the moon.

He hadn't anticipated sex becoming an issue between them; hadn't anticipated sex ever being an issue in his *life* again. And although he couldn't say with any degree of honesty that the sensation of physically wanting a woman again was unpleasant, it did put a new spin on this arranged-marriage idea. And an added danger he could do without.

It didn't take Chase long to pull on his jeans and a pale denim shirt, and when he finally left a few minutes later, he did so without so much as a backward glance.

Almost as though he couldn't get out of there fast enough, Skye thought with faint amusement.

Not surprisingly. His little game had almost gotten away from him this morning. And Chase McConnell didn't like it one bit.

Not, heaven knows, that she was in much better shape.

She drew in a careful breath, relieved that her heartbeat had returned to near normal finally. She felt as if she'd been hit by a truck, wandering around in a daze but remembering very little of the actual impact.

Annie had come bursting in with breakfast—she could recall that much. And Chase, obviously wanting to reinforce the myth of connubial bliss, had dived into bed and had started kissing her...but after that, it got all fuzzy.

She'd started out determined to strenuously protest, then had decided to go along with it so she'd have some leverage with which to barter her freedom. And then... something had happened. Something wonderful and unexpected and terrifying.

Which, she thought a little uneasily as she got out of bed and walked into the bathroom, made it all the more imperative that she convince Chase that this whole fake marriage thing wasn't going to work....

She took her time in the shower, dawdling under the powerful spray until the water was distinctly cool, then taking even more time to dry her thick hair. Getting dressed seemed to take twice as long as normal, too, although she could blame part of that on Annie, who had unpacked her things and put them away seemingly at random throughout the big room.

But finally she couldn't postpone it any longer. Taking a deep, fortifying breath, she picked up the untouched breakfast tray and pulled the bedroom door open, and headed downstairs to face her first full day as Chase McConnell's new wife.

By the expression on Sarah's young face when Skye walked into the kitchen, she knew the girl had been waiting expectantly for her. Setting the tray on the counter, she felt a twinge of guilt as she looked at the clock. "I had no idea it was so late! Good morning, Sarah...Annie."

Sarah's smile was radiant. "Good morning! Dad came down a long time ago but said I wasn't s'posed to go up and bother you."

From the other side of the kitchen, where she was standing behind the massive island rolling pastry, Annie eyed Skye speculatively. "You going to sleep in this late every morning? Most people around here have got half a day's work done by this hour."

Skye held Annie's stare evenly, deciding if she didn't set some boundaries right now this was only going to get worse. She could sympathize with the older woman, who obviously felt hurt and resentful that Chase had kept the news of his impending marriage from her. As an important member of the McConnell household, she deserved better treatment.

But, Skye reminded herself, the situation was intolerable enough without having to suffer Annie's abuse on top of it. "Nine o'clock is late," she said firmly, "but hardly a hanging offense. Even on the Rocking M."

Annie's mouth pursed. "Coffee's hot. I made pancakes for Chase. Or there's eggs and bacon or—"

"Coffee's fine, thanks," Skye said quietly, pouring herself a cup. There was a basket of fruit on the side table and she helped herself to an orange, then rummaged through the drawers and cupboards until she found a knife and a small plate. Then she walked across to the big round oak table in the bay window and sat down across from Sarah. "So, are you going to show me around the ranch today?"

Sarah nodded vigorously. Her shoulder-length hair was the color of winter wheat, more silver than gold, and was held back with a blue ribbon that matched the clear cerulean of her eyes. She was an incredibly pretty child, with her father's wide, clear eyes and firm mouth, but there were circles under her eyes, and she looked tired and a little drawn.

"Or," Skye put in thoughtfully, "we could just sort of hang around today and take it easy."

Sarah's face fell, but only momentarily. "We could go out to the pond," she offered. "And one of the mares had a foal two days ago—we can look at it. And Desdemona had kittens." She looked at Skye a little worriedly. "You *do* like cats, don't you?"

"I love cats. Who's Desdemona?"

"She was Miss Joanne's cat," Annie put in tartly. "Brought her all the way over from her parents' place when she moved in here."

"She's my cat now, Annie."

Annie's face softened. "Yes, honey, she is at that. And a lovely cat, too. Even if she doesn't have very good taste in the gentlemen she attracts."

Sarah rolled her eyes. "Annie! We can't be *sure* Romeo is the father."

Annie's mouth twitched with what Skye thought might actually turn into a smile given a little time.

"Honey, every one of them four kittens is the spitting image of old Romeo, right down to the crook in its tail."

Sarah traded a smile with Skye. "You can pick one if you want. To be *your* cat, I mean. Dad says we've gotta give them all away, then he's taking Desdemona to the vet so she can't have anymore."

"Now don't you go roaming off, missy," Annie put in. "That physiotherapist lady is coming again today."

Sarah made a face. "Can't she come tomorrow? This is Skye's first day here!" She toyed with her glass of juice. "Did...umm...Dad tell you about my leg?"

"Just a bit," Skye said casually, thinking about the crutches she'd seen in Sarah's room last night. And the heavy brace lying discarded nearby. "He thought you'd want to tell me about it yourself." It was a blatant lie— Chase had told her nothing about the extent of Sarah's injuries—but if the medical bills he was facing were any indication, they were pretty severe.

"I fell off a horse," Sarah said simply. "Dad thinks it was his fault, but it wasn't. I was in a coma for a whole *week*." She smiled with obvious pride. "There was a bunch of stuff wrong with my back and my leg. I've had four operations already, and I don't need crutches anymore." She grinned widely, the gap where she'd lost a tooth giving her a gamin look. "I have to use a cane and I can't walk for too long, but Daddy says after the next operation, I'll be almost as good as new."

"She wears out easy," Annie put in with a warning look at Skye. "The doctors don't want her putting too much strain on that leg until it heals a bit more."

"Well," Skye said smoothly, "I'm sure we can manage just fine. But I *don't* think putting the physiotherapist off is a good idea."

Sarah looked unhappy. "Please? Just a day? It really *hurts.*"

"I know. I tore up my knee skiing a few years ago and needed surgery. After the cast came off I had to go to physio every day for nearly three weeks."

"Did it hurt?"

"I yelled my head off every time she came near me!"

"Really?" Sarah's face brightened. "Did you really?"

"They used to have to close the windows in case people called the police," Skye said with a grin.

Sarah giggled. "Me, too. Daddy can't even stand being in the house when the therapist is here. He rides up to Mary's Mountain just so he doesn't have to listen."

Skye felt her heart give a sudden twist of sympathy, not so much for this blue-eyed little girl who seemed to be taking the surgery and pain in stride, but for the remote, closed man who seemed to think it was his fault. "Well, I'll tell you what—we'll hold hands this afternoon when she works on your leg, and when it hurts, we'll both just yell as hard as we can, how's that?"

Sarah's eyes widened. "Yeah! We'll make so much noise we'll shake the shingles!" She laughed, looking around at Annie. "That's what you always used to say before my accident, wasn't it, Annie? That when I played in the house, I'd shake the shingles."

"Yes, honey," Annie said with a gentle smile, her eyes filled with such love it made Skye's breath catch. "And I'll gladly put up with them shingles shaking right clean off the roof if it means you're getting better." Then, as though suddenly aware of Skye's sympathetic gaze, she banged a mound of pastry down on the countertop and began rolling it out furiously, flour lifting in a haze around her.

Sarah made a face, then giggled into her apple juice, her eyes glowing with mischief. And Skye, feeling torn between laughter and tears, carefully started peeling her orange.

Chase was through the kitchen door and halfway across to the counter where Annie always kept a pot of coffee on the go before he realized Skye was there. He paused, contemplating retreat.

Then decided not to. He'd started this, he reminded himself as he took down a glazed earthenware mug and filled it with steaming coffee. He carried the coffee across to the table, feeling his gut tighten up at the sight of her, and distracted himself by grinning broadly at his daughter instead. "You still here? I thought you'd finished that juice two hours ago."

"I was waiting for Skye to come down. Hug?"

"Hug." Scooping Sarah up in one arm, he gave her a ferocious hug, noticing, as he always did, how light she was. How fragile and tiny. He rested his cheek against her sweet-scented hair for a long moment, swallowing a sudden thickness in his throat, then let her slide to the floor. "Your therapist is coming today, isn't she?"

"Yeah." Sarah's nose wrinkled with disgust. "Skye says she'll help me yell, though."

"Help you *yell?*" Bemused, he eased one of the chairs around and straddled it carelessly, resting his arms across the back. And, finally, he let himself look at Skye.

There was a hint of color in her cheeks he could have sworn hadn't been there when he'd first come in, and she seemed almost to brace herself for his eye contact.

"Nothing hurts as much when you've got some company," she said calmly.

He just nodded, taking a sip of too-hot coffee to have an excuse to look away.

"I'm taking Skye out to the pond, Dad. Do you want to come?"

"No." His voice was slightly rough. He took another swallow of the coffee, then pushed the mug aside and uncoiled to his feet.

"And don't you go wearing yourself out. You know what the doc said."

"Da-ad!" She drew the word into two long disapproving syllables and gave him a look that spoke volumes. "Honestly! You'd think I was a little kid or something."

"You are a little kid," Chase teased, reaching out to tweak her nose. "A very special little kid. I'll see you later."

She grinned up at him. "You haven't kissed Skye yet."

Chase swore under his breath. He'd been trying so hard to ignore the effect Skye was having on him that he'd forgotten she was *supposed* to be having this effect on him.

"That's right, handsome." Skye was leaning well back in her chair, gazing up at him with a thoroughly malicious smile.

She was enjoying this, he realized with sudden annoyance. What had happened between them this morning had shaken her up, all right, but knowing she was affecting him like this gave her an advantage—and she knew it.

And she was too damn smart not to use it if she thought it might get her out of this fake marriage any quicker.

Which was not going to happen, he advised her silently. He smiled back at her. "Well, I guess I can fix that fast enough." Tipping his hat onto the back of his head, he cupped her chin in his hand and lifted her face, and, before she could do more than draw in a startled little breath, he'd planted his mouth firmly over hers.

He breached the barricade of half-parted lips with a single thrust of his tongue and kissed her aggressively, deciding to teach her a lesson once and for all. She was sweet with the flavor of oranges, and as he captured her tongue with his and teased her into responding, he could feel her fingers curl where she was gripping his arm.

It threatened to get away from him in the end. His body responded not just to the promise in the kiss but to the memory of having her in his arms only a couple of hours ago, and when he finally lifted his mouth from hers they were both breathing unsteadily.

"Careful, Red," he murmured, nuzzling her ear. "Try that again and you could just find yourself with a hell of a lot more on your hands than you'd counted on." Straightening, he smiled down at her. "See you later, sweetheart."

Not if she could help it, Skye thought dizzily, fighting to catch her breath as she watched him stroll nonchalantly toward the door, all long legs and broad shoulders and that aura of infuriating male arrogance. Damn it, when was she going to learn? Trying to outfox Chase McConnell at his own game was *not* going to work.

The back door opened again and she glanced around in mild panic, wondering what he wanted now. But to her relief, it wasn't Chase. The newcomer was an older man, a little portly and running to gray, with a bushy mustache and a broad grin that stretched nearly ear to ear when he saw her.

"Well, I'll be damned! Sorry, Mother," he added hastily, glancing in Annie's direction. Sweeping his hat off, he strode toward Skye, hand extended. "Name's Tom. Tom Lindquist. And I've been bustin' a gut ever since Chase called yesterday to say he got hisself hitched."

His warmth was so sincere it would have been impossible not to get caught up in it. Skye stood up with a smile and took his hand, and in the next instant found herself swept into a hug as enthusiastic as the man himself.

"Thomas, quit making a fool of yourself."

He stepped back, still grinning broadly, and looked Skye up and down with a stockman's eye. What he saw obviously pleased him. He nodded and slapped his denimed thigh.

"A thoroughbred, by God! Good legs, good conformation—and look at that hair! You're a damn fine-lookin' woman, missus." His eyes twinkled. "But then Chase always did have an eye for a good horse and a good woman. His daddy taught him that." He gave Skye a broad wink. "'Course, I had a hand in it, too."

"Thomas!" Annie's voice whipped across the kitchen. "If you have nothing better to do, you can bring in some wood for the fireplace. And that back screen door needs looking at, too."

"It'll have to wait, Mother. I'm helping Chase fix the corral gate where that bone-head chestnut gelding broke through it last week." He cocked a grin at Skye. "That horse ain't the man he used to be, but every now and again—when the moon's just right—he scents himself a mare and starts actin' foolish."

"Thomas!"

"Lord, there's no resting when she's on the warpath," he said in a conspiratorial mutter.

"I heard that, old man! And I ain't even *close* to being on the warpath yet." The rolling pin hit the counter for emphasis. "And this kitchen ain't a town meeting hall!"

"I think," Skye said, looking around at Sarah, "that we should go for that walk now."

Five

It was only when she got up from the table that Sarah's full disability was painfully obvious. The denim coveralls she was wearing couldn't hide the awkward twist to her right leg, and when she walked, it dragged clumsily. The cane helped—Skye doubted she'd be able to walk without it—but even the short distance from the back door to the edge of the yard left the girl panting and a little pale.

"Sarah, how far did you say the pond was?"

"Not too far," Sarah said hopefully. "Please, Skye? Please? I haven't been down there all spring. Hamlet's back, and I haven't even seen him!"

"Hamlet?" Skye had to laugh as she unlatched the gate. "Someone in your family likes Shakespeare."

"That was my mom. Annie says she liked reading a lot."

Skye nodded, latching the gate behind them and strolling alongside Sarah. The air was clear and cool, with just a hint of the day's heat in it, and it bubbled through Skye like a good wine.

Long, rolling foothills lifted around them, dotted with fir and ponderosa pine, and here and there an outcrop of rock jutted up from the pale golden grass like a wind-worn temple.

On a nearby hillside, a small herd of horses grazed peacefully, and Skye smiled as she watched a couple of gawky foals gallop around on their spidery legs. No two ways about it: the Rocking M ranch was, all hostility toward its owner aside, one of the most beautiful pieces of country she'd seen in a long while.

Jack, Sarah's black-and-white collie, settled in beside her, tongue lolling, and now and again he'd glance at her with an almost proprietorial wag of his bushy tail as though to see if she approved of things.

They made slow progress, following the path that wound in and out of groves of trees along the edge of a small tinkling creek. It was hard going for Sarah in places, but she seemed fine as long as they rested often along the way. She was so filled with eagerness that Skye didn't have the heart to suggest they turn back.

"Sarah, you've…well, weren't you worried about your dad bringing home a new wife? Especially one you'd never even met?"

Sarah grinned cheerfully. "Annie was worried, but not me. I knew you had to be nice. Dad wouldn't marry anyone who wasn't."

Skye cursed Chase McConnell silently. He was going to destroy that wonderful trust without even knowing it. By the time this was over, Sarah would never be quite this open again, this vulnerable.

"I don't remember my mother very well," Sarah said after a moment. "I was just four when she died. I mean, I *remember* her, but not..." She shrugged. "Dad won't talk about her."

"Never?"

"Annie says he packed all her things away after the accident. He won't even let Annie put her picture out. And I have to keep Desdemona in the barn. Although," she added with a sly glance at Skye, "I sneak her in lots of times. It's like the necklace I have of Mom's—I have to hide it, or he'd take it away."

She concentrated on her footing on the rough ground. "Annie says it makes him too sad. I ask him to tell me about her sometimes, because it's getting harder and harder to remember her and I'm scared that one day—" She stopped and looked up at Skye, her expression desolate. "If you forget what someone looks like, does that mean you don't love them anymore?"

Tears caught at the back of Skye's throat without warning, catching her so by surprise she had to swallow, hard, before even attempting to answer. "It just means the picture in your mind is fading, that's all. You'll always love your mother—you think about her and you talk about her. That's part of loving her."

Sarah nodded slowly, as though not entirely convinced.

"Don't you have a picture of her? Of your own, I mean?"

"Daddy took them all away after she died," Sarah whispered.

Damn you, Chase McConnell, Skye thought furiously. What the *hell* right do you have to destroy your daughter's memories of her mother just because you can't bear the pain of losing her?

She was still thinking about this—and still angry—when they reached the pond a few minutes later.

It was, as Skye had suspected, considerably farther from the house than Sarah had let on, lying in a boggy spot where the stream petered out into marshland. The pond itself was a small oval of water that mirrored the sky, surrounded on three sides by reeds filled with birds and trilling frogs. The open side was dry ground, and as they strolled along it, Skye could make out hundreds of tiny bird tracks embroidering the mud at the edge of the water.

A squadron of brown ducks clattered by, the drake looking as proud of his harem as any sultan, and in the distance two white swans glided across the still water like hand-blown figurines.

"There he is! There's Hamlet!" Sarah pointed at a black-and-gray Canada goose drifting out from behind a wall of reeds, looking slightly bedraggled and a little lost.

"Poor Hamlet. He and Ophelia have come to our pond to raise their babies for years and years. But this year Hamlet was over a month late, and Ophelia still hasn't come." Sarah looked across at the bird sadly. "Dad says she probably got hurt or something. And he says geese mate forever and that Hamlet will be alone now."

Skye dropped her arm around the girl's shoulders and gave her a hug, thinking idly that Hamlet and Chase were two of a kind in a way: both widowers, both determinedly alone, both bewildered by an unfair world and slightly lost.

"He might?" she heard herself saying, wondering if she was talking about the man or the goose. "I'm sure even geese get lonely, Sarah. He may not think he wants another Ophelia, but one day he might find her by accident and be happy again."

"Do you think so?" Sarah looked up at her with a faint spark of hope in her eyes. "Dad found you, after all. So maybe Hamlet *will* find another Ophelia."

And Skye, watching the old bird drift in aimless circles, felt something start to ache inside her.

"You're *what?*" Phil Duggan's voice came snapping out of the telephone receiver, vibrant with disbelief.

"I said I'm married."

There was a long, taut silence. "Since when?"

"Three days ago." Or half a lifetime, Chase thought, depending on how you viewed it. He was leaning against the wall by the window in the kitchen, and he moved the pale yellow curtain aside with his finger to look out to where Skye and Sarah were sitting at the picnic table in the backyard. They had their heads together, pale gold tipped against flame red, and he could see Sarah frowning as she slowly read from the book in front of her.

That was one thing in Skye's favor, he had to admit. She might be driving *him* out of his mind, but in the three days she'd been here, she'd somehow managed to reignite Sarah's interest in her schoolwork where neither he nor Annie had been successful.

"Is it—" Duggan broke off, laughing softly. "I was going to ask you if it was legal. But you wouldn't knowingly do something illegal, would you, Chase? So there's no need to ask, right?"

"Right." And that's what it had come down to, Chase thought wearily. To where he was lying to one of his oldest friends. And his lawyer, to boot.

"Who's the lucky bride?"

"You don't know her. She's from Portland. A teacher." And the sexiest damn thing he'd met in a long while, Chase added to himself, watching as Skye lifted her head and laughed, the sunlight cascading off her glowing mane of hair. He gave himself a shake and tried to concentrate.

"That's a point in my favor, too, isn't it? That she's a teacher?"

"Oh, yeah," Duggan said in a resigned tone. "What's this all about, Chase? How long have you known this woman? When did you—"

"It's a long story, Phil."

"I'll just bet it is."

"You were the one who suggested it."

There was another pause, then the sound of a soft, weary oath. "Okay. No more questions. I'll put it in my report. And Chase..."

"Yeah?"

"Just be careful, old buddy. The ice is pretty damn thin that far out." He paused. "Make sure there are *no* loose ends left lying around, do you get what I'm saying? I have to believe this marriage is on the up and up because that's what you've told me, but Tup Hewitt and his people are going to be mighty suspicious. That means they'll be snooping around, trying to discredit you. So whatever you're doing out there, make it watertight."

"I appreciate the advice, Counselor."

"I'm sure." Duggan sounded bemused. "I'll be around later with some papers you need to sign for the Mary's Mountain deal. I'm...uh...looking forward to meeting your *wife.*"

Chase hung up the receiver and reached for the mug of coffee at his elbow, taking a deep swallow as he watched Skye and Sarah suddenly dissolve into laughter. He felt something give a little tug inside him, seeing Sarah so exuberant and animated.

When was the last time he'd spent an hour or two with her, just the two of them, like in the old days when he'd take her riding or fishing or catching fireflies in the dusk...?

He swore and rubbed his eyes wearily, then finished his coffee in one long swallow. If nothing else came out of this pretend marriage, at least Sarah was getting a couple of weeks of companionship and laughter. And when Skye left? Well, he'd figure that out when he came to it. Sarah would understand.

He frowned, thinking he should be getting back outside to help Tom unload that truckful of oats. And there were three hundred bales of clover hay and another two hundred of bedding straw that needed stacking in the barn, not to mention a loading chute that needed repairing after one of those three bulls he'd sold last week had smashed its way through it.

And there were the other never-ending chores: sixty miles of barbed wire that needed stringing, corral fences that needed repair, storage sheds that needed building, stock that needed checking. The work hadn't disappeared just because he'd had to let all the hired hands go.

But he found himself just standing there, shoulder against the window frame, watching Skye and his daughter.

Skye mostly, he admitted with a wry smile. And she was damned easy to look at, no doubt about that, small and compact and as tidy as a cat, with that unruly mane of red hair and those snapping eyes that made his breath catch when they met his unexpectedly. She always smelled of shampoo and fresh air and honeysuckle soap, and lately he'd found himself making excuses to get close to her just to breathe it in. Making excuses to touch her, too.

Which hadn't been part of the plan, damn it. He shoved himself away from the window and strode across to the door, settling his hat into its customary angle and trying to put Skye out of his mind. And last night's dream, too, while he was at it.

Not that last night's dream had been any different from the ones he'd been having ever since he'd brought her here. His nights were filled with them, hot, erotic dreams that left him aroused and angry and confused.

Wanting and not wanting her with the same urgency, he hated himself for the weakness that made him lie in the darkness of the bedroom, listening to her soft breathing and fantasizing about making love to her. Feeling every touch and caress and deep, hungry kiss as though it were real, knowing exactly what it would be like, driving himself crazy.

And the whole time, knowing that he was somehow betraying Joanne. That if they hadn't had that argument that afternoon, if she hadn't gone into town in the old truck by herself, if he'd been driving when the brakes had given way... if, if, if.

Three days. Skye managed a faint smile as she wandered into the big country kitchen, feeling restless and bored and at loose ends. It was hard to believe she'd been here for three days, settling into the role of dutiful, sweet wife more easily than she could ever have imagined.

Almost too easily. She poured herself a cup of coffee and added a generous splash of cream. There were moments—just flickers of time, really—when it almost seemed real. When she'd catch herself feeling the sense of *belonging* that she imagined a real wife would feel.

And feelings like those were dangerous. Because this wasn't real. In another week and a half she'd walk out of these people's lives and that would be the end of it. Sarah. Chase. Even Annie. They'd just be memories by the time the summer was over, players in a brief interlude that had started out as a nightmare and had quickly become a study in wishful thinking.

It was all here—all she'd ever dreamed of. The handsome husband, the beautiful daughter, the house, the ranch . . . all so perfect they could have been taken straight from her teenage fantasies, part of the blueprint to the *ordinary* life she'd always wanted.

And now that she had it, it wasn't even real.

There was a slight noise behind her and Skye glanced around just as Chase stepped into the kitchen. He paused as though startled to see her there, then nodded a little cautiously and walked across to the sink, lean hipped and ruggedly masculine in those damned tight jeans that hugged his buttocks and thighs like an old friend. There was something about him that seemed to fill any room he was in with a raw male energy that always made her feel a little weak-kneed, and she found her gaze drawn to him helplessly.

It wasn't until he turned the cold water on and held his left hand under it that she realized he was hurt.

"What on earth did you do!" Putting the coffee down, she walked across to him, her stomach knotting when she saw the trickle of blood running down his hand and dripping into the sink.

"I was cutting the wire on a bale of straw and nicked myself," he muttered. "Went right through the damn glove."

She reached out and grasped his hand, turning it toward her. He'd sliced the fleshy pad on the outside of his hand deeply, and blood dripped between her fingers. "That's no nick—it needs stitches!"

"A chunk of adhesive tape will hold it together. There's some under the sink somewhere. Annie keeps stuff like that handy."

"If you're in the habit of doing this to yourself, I can see why." Skye knelt on the floor and started rummaging through the cupboard under the sink. Finding a plastic box with some first-aid supplies in it, she stood up and poked through it, exclaiming with satisfaction when she discovered a bottle of hydrogen peroxide. "Okay, hold out your hand...."

"What is that?" he asked suspiciously.

Skye arched an eyebrow and looked up at him, finding those silvery gray eyes unsettlingly close. "You do the bleeding, I'll do the mending, all right?"

A flicker of a smile touched his mouth and he shoved his hat back, his eyes amused. "Bossy little thing, aren't you?"

"That's what you get when you pick your wife out of the lineup at the local jail."

Chase gave a snort of laughter. He smelled of horses and hay and hot, clean sweat, and her heart gave a distracting little thud before she was able to get her concentration hauled back to the gash on his hand. She turned his palm up and carefully poured a healthy splash of peroxide over the cut, trying not to notice how their bodies touched when she leaned over the sink.

And realized, in the same instant, that she was also giving him a perfect view straight down the front of her shirt. She straightened hastily and gave him an accusing look, and found him grinning broadly.

"Man enough to look," he drawled, eyes glinting with deviltry, "and gentleman enough not to mention it."

"Until you get caught!"

"Honey, you put something that pretty in front of a man, he'd have to be blind—or a damned fool—not to notice."

"So much for the cowboy code of honor!"

The lazy grin widened. "Hell, that just means if I caught someone *else* looking, I'd have to punch him in the mouth."

It was impossible not to laugh, and for some reason she didn't feel even half as indignant as she probably should have. She pulled a towel off the rack and wrapped it around his hand. "Hold that for a minute while I cut some tape."

"Where is everyone?"

"Annie's gone into town for groceries, and Sarah's having a nap. Her leg was bothering her a bit."

"Bad?" His voice sharpened. "Should I give her doc a call?"

Skye looked up at him, her heart giving a little twist at the sudden anxiety in his face and eyes. "No, it's nothing serious. She just pushes herself too hard sometimes. And this was my fault. She's been dying to show me those three new foals in the west pasture and I foolishly let her take me out there. It's farther than I thought."

"Farther than she let on, you mean," he said with a hint of wry amusement in his voice. "Damn, she's stubborn!"

"I can't imagine where she gets it from."

He had one hip braced against the edge of the sink and was gazing down at her, a lazy smile toying around his mouth. "Not that you'd recognize stubborn when you saw it or anything."

"Me? Uh-uh. Never." Frowning in concentration, she unwrapped his hand and motioned him to hold it over the sink again. Carefully she pressed the edges of the cut together, then taped two strips of adhesive across it and carefully pressed a sterile pad against it. "Hold this."

He did so, and she cut off four more strips of tape to hold the pad firmly, then anchored the entire thing by winding a length of gauze around his hand and tying it securely. "That will keep it clean. Take the gauze off at night so the air gets to it, and I'll change the dressing a couple of times a day."

"You're handy to have around."

"I got my first taste of kitchen first aid early," she said quietly, capping the peroxide bottle and starting to rewind the gauze. "Not all the marches and demonstrations my parents were in were peaceful. No matter where we lived, our place always seemed to turn into a drop-in center, and I can remember seeing kids lying on our living room floor, bleeding and crying after a run-in with the National Guard or the police or looters or what have you."

"I was listening last night when you were telling Sarah about growing up in that Volkswagen camper, traveling all over. Sounds like you had a hell of a childhood."

"It's improved with the telling." She smiled fleetingly. "At the time, all I wanted was to be normal. I hated it when people pointed at us and called us dirty hippies, and never staying in one place long enough for me to make friends. And I'd have given my right arm to have a normal mother who baked cookies instead of getting arrested."

A lazy smile canted his mouth to one side and Skye had to laugh. "Okay, okay. But those two hours Ives had me locked up were the first time *I've* ever been behind bars!"

"What are they doing now? Still fighting the good fight?"

"On and off. They run an organic health food store up in Washington, but they still get involved in the occasional 'cause'. My mother's name is still Meadow Buttercup and she and my dad still aren't married, but they're pretty respectable citizens now, paying taxes and a mortgage like real people." She smiled. "Dad still belongs to the old SunShine Coalition, of course, but—"

"The SunShine *what?*"

Skye had to laugh again. "Oh, it was just one of my dad's dreams. He figured there was power in numbers, and that if all the activist movements that were around at the time worked together, they could move mountains. So he and some friends put together the Coalition. It was supposed to coordinate all these groups into a common cause. It worked for a while, but then they all got political and started going their own ways."

"Seems to me they still managed to move a mountain or two."

"Yeah." Skye smiled reminiscently. "It's still around—the Coalition, I mean. But it's hard to get people worked up for a cause these days. Not like back then, anyway."

"You sound as though you miss it."

Skye shrugged, snapping the lid back on the adhesive tape and putting the things into the plastic box. "Sometimes I think I must disappoint my parents. They were part of a movement that changed an entire country if you think about it. They *did* things, important things. They made a difference."

"You're making a difference," Chase said very softly. His gaze moved across her face, feature by feature, as though seeing something there that fascinated him. "I guess I've been so busy giving you a hard time I haven't bothered to tell you that...."

He reached out and touched her cheek with the back of his hand and Skye went very still, feeling a little dizzy. His face was close ... so close she could see the fine spray of white lines at the outer corners of his eyes where he squinted against the sun, a smudge of dust on his forehead where he'd wiped it with his arm, the odd little flecks of brown in his eyes.

And his mouth, so strong and unyielding, almost hard at one moment and softly coaxing the next . . . *that* mouth was dipping toward hers and she lifted hers to meet it, mesmerized by the warmth and nearness of him, by the decidedly dangerous things she saw in his eyes as they held hers. . . .

Those eyes held hers for a moment longer, a little quizzical, a little bemused. And then they drew back almost reluctantly and she wondered if she'd only imagined he'd been going to kiss her.

"You make a pretty good wife, Red." He held up his hand and flexed his fingers.

"And you don't make a half-bad husband."

He looked at her, almost surprised, then a smile played around one corner of his mouth. "I'm a little rusty at it, but most of it's coming back."

Watching him, Skye felt a pang of something that felt almost like regret. And she found herself thinking, very idly, that there could be worse things than living in this house and looking across a room and seeing this man and knowing he was yours. Fleetingly she thought of Joanne. Of how lucky she'd been to have the reality.

There was the sound of a car door banging closed just then, and Chase roused himself. "That'll be Annie."

"Yes." It would be the easiest thing in the world, she found herself thinking in that moment, to fall in love with this man. To convince herself that all the pretending meant something real.

And then the back door opened and Annie strode into the kitchen and the spell was broken. Chase frowned and resettled his hat low on his forehead, muttering something that sounded like "thanks" as he headed for the door, and she just smiled at his retreating back.

Annie gave a sniff. "Nice that *some* of us have got time to lollygag around drinking coffee in the middle of the day."

"I just spent two hours weeding those rose beds at the front of the house," Skye said with a hint of irritation.

"Those were Miss Joanne's roses." Annie's tone made it clear that she didn't think Skye had any right to be near them. "She planted every one of them bushes. Knew the names of them, too."

"Hurray for Joanne," Skye muttered, immediately feeling ashamed of her hostility toward a woman she'd never even known.

"Don't you go getting smart on me, missy. I know all about you, you know. You're not getting away with anything."

I'm getting away with more than you think, Skye very nearly said, then decided to keep her mouth shut for a change.

"You think you can pull the wool over my eyes like you have that poor man you finagled into marrying you?" Annie gave a snort. "*He* might be falling all over himself every time you wiggle that pretty little bottom at him, but I know trouble when I see it." She threw Skye a triumphant look. "I know your type, missy. After Joanne died, they were out here six deep, trying to get their hooks into the poor man before his wife was even decently buried."

"Annie . . . !"

"I see the way he looks at you, watching you every minute, practically pawing the dirt like a stallion next to a corralful of mares. But that's only because he's young and healthy, and it's been a long time since he's had a woman in *that* way. But all your sexy carrying-ons won't keep him blind forever, missy. I figure you must be pretty good in that department, too, the way he goes all glassy eyed whenever he looks at you. But he's a grown man, no foolish boy who can't think of anything but the ache in his jeans.''

Skye had managed to catch her breath finally, aware that her cheeks were scarlet. ''Annie, that's—''

''Oh, no. Sooner or later he's going to realize what I've known all along. That it ain't him—*or* what's in his jeans—that you're after. You want the money.''

''Money? What on earth are you—''

''Well, you're not going to get it, missy. That money's for the child, to get her walking again. And you can wiggle that perky little bottom until it falls right off, but Chase ain't so starved for what you're giving him that he'll stay blind forever!''

It would have been funny, Skye found herself thinking, if the words hadn't been filled with such venom. She had her mouth open for a furious reply, then realized that she couldn't even defend herself. Not without giving the whole thing away.

Tears of anger and frustration filled her eyes and she wheeled away and strode across to the kitchen door and out into the afternoon sunshine without saying a thing.

She didn't realize that Chase was in the barn until it was too late. Coming into the dim interior from the bright sunlight and half-blinded by tears, she didn't see him until he moved. She stopped, not knowing whether to keep going or to make a hasty retreat.

He was stacking bales of straw, and the air around him shimmered like gold in the bars of sunlight slanting down from the loft above him. He'd stripped to the waist and the bronzed planes of his back and shoulders gleamed with sweat, jeweled with bits of straw and dust, and each time he picked up a bale and swung it up and around, the muscles in his back would writhe and knot.

Without even intending to, she found herself remembering the way that same lean, muscular body had felt lying in her arms the other morning. His skin had been as smooth and warm as heated gold and he'd moved against her with restrained power and she could distinctly recall the strength in the arms cradling her, the treacherous thoughts that had filled her mind as she'd lain pressed tightly against him and had—

Chase glanced around just then, as though suddenly aware that someone was watching him, and as his gaze collided with hers, Skye felt a hot blush rush up from the collar of her shirt. Caught there with no easy retreat, she froze for a moment, her mind blank, aware of nothing but the incriminating heat on her cheeks.

He straightened and wiped the sweat from his face with one corded forearm.

"I...the kittens," she stammered, wishing her heart would quit bouncing around like a ping-pong ball. "I came to see the kittens."

She looked as though he'd just walked in and caught her with her hand in the cookie jar, Chase thought with amusement, her cheeks flaming almost as scarlet as that wondrous red hair that never ceased to fascinate him.

And he realized, very suddenly, that she'd been standing there watching him. Liking what she saw, perhaps. Maybe even thinking one or two of the kinds of things he'd caught himself thinking lately, his mind wandering in all sorts of directions, all of them to do with her and all of them as dangerous as hell. . . .

He thought of standing in the kitchen with her not half an hour ago and thinking some of those same things. Just before he'd come *this* close to kissing her.

It made his stomach tighten just slightly and he found himself staring at her deliberately, taunting himself with her. With everything that just seeing her did to him and made him feel.

Abruptly, half-afraid of what would happen if he didn't break off whatever was going on between them, he walked across to a galvanized bucket sitting on a nearby bale. Scooping up a handful of water in his cupped palms, he drank deeply, then splashed the rest on his face, sweeping his hat off and shaking himself like a dog, water spraying. He ran his wet hands through his hair, then wiped his mouth with his arm and retrieved his discarded shirt from the nail where it was hanging and crumpled it into a ball and toweled his chest and shoulders with it.

And then, finally, he let himself look at her again. "Annie must be on the warpath. When I was a kid, I'd hide out from her in here, too."

She smiled—that smile that always made his breath catch, and he forced himself to look away, tossing his shirt over the side of a stall.

"Did it work?"

"Depended on how much trouble I was in. There were a couple of times she came roaring out here after me and dragged me back into the house to face the music."

Skye laughed and strolled a little nearer, the sunbeams streaming down from the loft just above her glittering and sparkling over her hair. "I have a feeling that if she ever discovers you're lying about this marriage, you may be out here permanently."

Chase winced. "That bad?"

"She's been a member of this family for a long time, and she's hurt that you're shutting her out now. That you brought me here without even telling her you were thinking of marrying again."

"I wasn't," Chase reminded her dryly.

"Yeah, well, you're going to have to do some pretty fancy talking to make things up to her when this is all over." She smiled at him as she walked across to the ladder leading up to the loft. "I'm just glad I don't have to live with her, McConnell."

"So marry me, and we can tell her the whole thing."

"I'm already married to you, remember? For the next week and a half, anyway."

"I meant really marry me." He said it just to see her reaction. And maybe, in a way, to see his own.

She stood with one foot on the bottom rung of the ladder, her face mirroring bewilderment. "What are you talking about now?"

Casually Chase strolled toward her, thumbs hooked in the waistband of his jeans. "We get along pretty well, all considered. Sarah thinks you're the best thing to come along since boys, and Annie—after the fireworks die down—will approve just because she doesn't think it's good for a man to be single too long."

"You're dangerous, you know that?" Her eyes flashed slightly as she said it. "I've never met anybody who could come up with more off-the-wall ideas! Just where does what *I* want fit into this wonderful scheme?"

"I don't know, Red." He leaned one shoulder against the ladder and stared down at her, almost daring her. "What *do* you want?"

"A heck of a lot more than a make-believe marriage to *you!*"

"It wouldn't be make-believe, Red," he said softly, his eyes holding hers. "It would be as real as they come."

For a split second, as her wide and softly green eyes locked with his, he wished it were possible to convince her to go through with it. It was one of those crazy ideas that had come out of nowhere, catching him unawares last night as he'd lain in the darkness, unable to sleep, listening to her soft breathing and wondering what it would be like to wake up every morning for the rest of his life with her beside him. And it had occurred to him that actually marrying her might not be such a bad idea at all.

In fact, in the dark silences of the night at two o'clock this morning, the idea had begun to take on a definite appeal.

To his surprise, it still did.

He grinned recklessly. "Hell, how can you turn it down?"

"I'd rather eat live bait, Mr. McConnell," she said very sweetly. "But thank you *so* much for asking."

Chase laughed lazily and stepped back as she started up the ladder. She made an intriguing picture as she climbed, and he didn't even pretend not to be interested. Her trim little backside was one of the prettiest sights he'd seen in a long while, and those long denim-clad legs were doing things to his imagination that should be outlawed.

It wasn't until she was nearly halfway up that she realized he was watching her and she faltered, suddenly self-conscious. Then she must have figured he was going to benefit from the show whether she kept going or came back down. She shot up the rest of the ladder as though on wings, and Chase couldn't keep from laughing again.

He didn't even know what made him decide to join her. He started back toward the straw bales with all the best intentions in the world, but in the next breath he found himself climbing the ladder, thinking a little idly that this was one sure way to get himself into more trouble than he needed.

Six

She was sitting cross-legged in a pile of hay with two of Desdemona's month old kittens in her lap. Chase paused at the top of the ladder, watching her, feeling a frisson of guilt work its way through him. He'd seen Joanne sit like that a hundred times, her blonde hair spilling around her shoulders, and yet—standing here watching Skye—he found himself thinking he'd never seen anything more beautiful.

And maybe that's what bothered him. Not that he thought of Joanne whenever he looked around at unexpected moments and saw Skye there—but that he *didn't* think of Joanne. That when he looked at Skye he *saw* Skye; when he wanted Skye, it was *her* he wanted, not the blonde-haired, blue-eyed woman he'd married and had once loved with every cell of his being. And it didn't seem right, damn it. What the hell kind of love had it been if he could forget that easily?

He swore softly to himself, confused by the strange welter of emotions taunting him, and suddenly wished he'd resisted the temptation to come up here.

Except that Skye glanced up just then and saw him standing there, and it was too late. An array of expressions flickered across her features, gone in a moment—the first had been undisguised pleasure, he was sure of it, then wariness, then what might have been faint apprehension.

"You look kind of shaken up," he said quietly, squatting on his heels beside her and reaching down to stroke one of the kittens. "Annie said something to you, didn't she?"

She shrugged a little too carelessly, not meeting his eyes.

Chase eased himself down beside her. "Want to talk about it?"

"Not particularly." She sounded angry and upset, Chase thought, but after a moment she tipped her head back and ran her hands through her mane of hair, raking it back from her face, and suddenly laughed.

"She thinks I'm using my female wiles to weasel my way into your bed—and your bank account. She informed me that you haven't had a sexual relationship in three years, which means you are at the mercy of your rampaging hormones. And me."

"She said *that?*"

"Among other things." Skye's eyes were filled with wry amusement. "She figures you'll come out of your daze anytime now and realize it's not your virile body I'm lusting after, but your ranch and your money. At least your cover story when I leave is in place. Just tell her you unmasked my true motives and threw me out."

"Damn it, that woman's gone too far this time!"

He started to lunge to his feet but Skye caught his arm. "Don't, Chase. She loves you and Sarah and she's fighting to protect you, that's all." She smiled ruefully. "I don't know why I let it bother me. In fact, I should be flattered she thinks I've got what it takes to turn a man's head."

"Don't sell yourself short, honey," he murmured, reaching out to take a piece of straw from her hair. "You've definitely got what it takes."

She looked a little startled.

"In fact," he added quietly, watching the way the dust motes hanging in the air shimmered around her like gold, "she's right about a lot of it. I haven't been with a woman since Joanne died. And my hormones have had quite a workout since you've been around."

She glanced at him, looking as surprised by the honesty of his admission as he was. There was a flicker of emotions in her eyes—confusion, pleasure, apprehension, maybe a hint of sadness—then she just frowned slightly and glanced away, looking uncertain.

What was he doing? he wondered idly. Seeing how close he could get to the fire without getting burned, or making a play for her? It had been a long while since he'd indulged in the social rituals with a woman—and if the expression of doubt on Skye's face was anything to go by, he was as rusty as hell.

Desdemona was sitting on a bale of straw, watching the kittens with maternal pride, and more to distract himself than anything, he gave the dumpy gray-and-white cat a pat. She turned her head and fixed him with a baleful emerald stare, and he winced, laughing. "Do you think she heard about that upcoming trip to the vet?"

"Maybe she's just feeling neglected."

She didn't say anything else, but she didn't need to. Chase winced again and reached out to run his hand down Desdemona's back. Joanne had brought the cat with her when they'd gotten married, and Des had slept at the foot of their bed every night for nearly four years. But after the accident, the cat's warm presence had seemed only to make his loss deeper, and he'd banished her to the barn.

The cat bumped her head against his hand suddenly and started to purr, and for some reason it gave Chase's heart a lift. One of the two kittens in Skye's lap was trying to wash its face, but it kept overbalancing and falling on its side, and finally it just stayed there and closed its eyes, yawning. "You've been helping Sarah with her reading."

"It would be a shame if she got so far behind in her schoolwork that she was held back." She smiled. "You got a very special daughter, McConnell."

"Why do you think I'm going to all this trouble to keep her?" He smiled fleetingly, rubbing Desdemona's chin. "She's going to miss you when this is over."

"I know. And I told you that would happen."

"If it's any consolation, I'm beginning to think you might have been right about a lot of it...."

Skye was silent for a long while, playing with the kitten. "This isn't—" Biting her lower lip, she glanced up at him again. "May I ask you something? Something... personal?"

Chase felt his stomach tighten slightly but ignored it, giving a snort of laughter. "Hell, I've told you about my sex life—or lack of it. What could be more personal than that?"

"What really happened to Sarah? I know she was thrown from a horse, but..." Her eyes held his searchingly. "There's more to it than that. I can see it on your face when you watch her. I can hear it in your voice when you talk about the accident. Something happened and you blame yourself, and it's tearing you apart."

It felt as though a band of steel had tightened around his chest and Chase had to struggle to catch his breath, fighting anger and guilt and shame. He started to get to his feet, intending to walk away and pretend she'd never asked the question. But he couldn't forget it, he reminded himself wearily. And there wasn't enough pretending in the whole world to make the pain go away.

"It was my fault that she got hurt," he heard himself say, his voice sounding thick and far away. "We were busy as hell with the new calf crop, branding and sorting. I'd been...numb. Operating on automatic, I guess, for the better part of two years. Sarah wanted to go out to the cemetery to put flowers on her mother's grave. I'd promised her we would just to keep her off my back about it, but this day she was real determined. I..." He swallowed and took his hat off, running his fingers through his hair and resting his bowed head in his hand. Forcing himself to remember.

"I hadn't been out there since the funeral. Couldn't face going out with Sarah. I put her off all day, telling her I was too busy. But she wouldn't let it go. I finally lost my temper and yelled at her, and she went storming off. She talked one of the hands into saddling her pony for her. She says she doesn't remember where she was going, but she wound up about twenty miles from here. Something spooked her pony and she was thrown into a pile of rock and scrub."

A slender hand appeared on his suddenly, her light touch gentler than anything he could remember. "It took us a couple of hours to even realize she was missing. Annie thought she was with me, and I figured she'd come back to the house. Then her pony came back in, lathered and hot, and we knew—" He had to stop to take a deep breath. "We went out after her, not even knowing where to start looking. It was old Jack who found her. She was...God, I thought she was dead. I remember looking down at her and going as cold as stone. Thinking I may as well just take my rifle and end it then and there because with her gone, I had nothing to live for.''

He didn't realize Skye had moved until he felt her small hand cup his bare shoulder, kneading at the stiffness there.

"They got her out by helicopter and flew her up to Portland. It was touch and go for nearly a week. I can remember sitting by that damned bed for days, alternating between profanity and prayers, so scared I was numb. All I could think of was that I'd betrayed Joanne. She'd left Sarah in my care, and I'd let her down.''

He looked up, his gaze holding Skye's; he felt haunted and cold. "I don't think I'd have held it together if she'd died. I lie awake nights sometimes, wondering what I would have done.''

"You can't keep blaming yourself," she said gently. "She needs you as badly as you need her, Chase. She needs your strength. When the therapist comes and you take off because you can't stand hearing her cry and knowing she's in pain, you're hurting her even more. *She* feels guilty—for making you feel bad, for driving you away. And she thinks you're angry with her.''

"Damn it, that's not what—''

"I know." Her fingers tightened on his shoulder. "I know, Chase. But Sarah's seven years old and she's scared to death she's going to lose you, too. I see it in her eyes every time you go out the door. She's terrified that you're going to just leave one day and not come back because of her. Because she reminds you of Joanne—and she knows how much pain that brings you.''

"I never thought..." He shook his head. "I know I'm not much of a father these days. Hell, maybe Hewitt's right...."

"No." Her voice was crisp. Almost angry. "You're a good father, Chase McConnell. And that child belongs here on the Rocking M, with you. Don't you *dare* start thinking about giving up now!''

The vehemence in her voice made him look up in surprise and she blushed, laughing softly. ''Sorry. I can never mind my own business. Give me a problem, and I jump right in.''

Chase found himself just looking at her, bemused. She wove powerful magic, this woman. It was as though she could look down inside him and see things he scarcely knew were there himself, could see where the hurts were and heal them. It had been a long time since he'd shared that much of himself with another person.

Skye drew in a deep breath and looked at him. ''I may as well get it all over with at once. I was going to talk to you about this later, but now's as good a time as any. A good friend of mine just outside Portland runs a summer day camp for kids Sarah's age. Karen's a nurse—she specialized in rehabilitation medicine before quitting to raise a family. I was wondering if...''

She bit her lower lip and looked at Chase as though trying to estimate his reaction. ''I was wondering if you'd let me take Sarah back with me, just until the summer's over. She says you have to take her up to Portland every few weeks anyway to check in with her doctors. Karen could do her physio, and I could help her with her schoolwork until she's caught up. I know most of the summer's gone, but it might keep her from feeling quite so... abandoned when I leave.

''And I was thinking,'' she added all in a rush, as though gaining courage from Chase's silence, ''that next spring, if she had that surgery in Portland as planned, she could spend a couple of months with me... if she wants to, of course. I could taxi her back and forth from the hospital for her checkups and so on. It would save you having to spend so much time away from the ranch and you'd know she was in good hands. I know Karen would be delighted to help. Between us, Sarah would have round-the-clock care with people she knows. It might make the whole ordeal a little easier.''

Chase stared at her, feeling as though he'd just been hit by a sandbag. "Where the hell did you come from, lady," he heard himself whisper.

Skye looked at him uncertainly. "I—I know I'm taking an awful lot for granted, but..." Shrugging, she let her gaze slip from his.

Chase took his hat off to rake his fingers through his hair, shaking his head. "When I brought you here, I just needed a temporary wife. I didn't expect something like this."

"Me, neither." She was frowning, looking at the kittens. "That first night here, I swore to myself that I was going to make you pay if I had to spend the next five years in court to do it. Then I met Sarah and..." She gave a helpless shrug again. "I didn't expect to wind up caring."

She said it with such quiet simplicity that it took Chase a moment to realize what she *had* said. He looked at her and found himself all tangled up in those sage green eyes, wondering what the hell was going on.

It was dim where they were sitting, the hot, still air glittering with motes of dust, and her eyes seemed very wide and very deep. She was wearing a white cotton shirt, sleeves rolled up to her elbows, collar open, and her skin gleamed with a light sheen of perspiration. A tendril of damp hair clung to the side of her throat, and before he even realized what he was doing, he'd reached out and had brushed it back with his finger, his hand very large and sun-browned against her fair skin.

And that's when he realized that it had just been a matter of time. If it hadn't been today, it would have been tomorrow or perhaps the next day. And if she hadn't come to him, he'd have gone after her. But one way or the other, sooner or later, this was destined to have happened....

And so it was with almost weary resignation that he lifted his hand to cup her face, then lowered his mouth to hers.

She didn't seem any more surprised than he was. Her hand skidded along his damp shoulder in a rough caress, and when he brushed his lips lightly across hers, they parted in welcome.

"I wasn't planning on this, either," he said roughly.

"I know."

Loving the scent of her skin, he drew his lips across her cheek and down the side of her throat, and she shivered slightly, then rested her cheek on his shoulder with a sigh.

"I want you." Chase brushed his palm across her breast, just a feather touch, but enough to feel her nipple tighten. "I want to be inside you, lady. I want to feel you all around me. I want you touching me. I want—" He nuzzled her throat, whispering things to her, things that made her moan softly, and when he cupped her breast again her breath hissed slightly and she moved deliberately against him, the nipple aroused and sensitive.

Her skin was moist and salty and he ran his tongue along the slope of her shoulder, pushing the collar of her shirt back. Her fingers brushed his thigh, so lightly it could have been an accident, but when he caught her hand and pressed it against his thigh and moved it slowly upward, he could feel her tremble.

Her eyes were heavy, and he read in them everything he needed and everything he wanted, realizing that he'd always known, somehow, that it was going to come to this.

There was no need to say anything more. Deliberately, holding her gaze intently, he slipped the top button on her shirt free, then the next. There were four, and as he undid the last one she hadn't moved, although her lips had parted just slightly and she was breathing more quickly.

Gently he drew the halves of the shirt apart with his hands, baring her lace-clad breasts, and he paused for a moment simply to look at her, feeling the blood starting to pound in his temples. Her breasts were smooth and milky above the cups of her bra, and he could see the outline of each full nipple through the fabric.

In no hurry, he bent lower and took one into his mouth, lace and all, and he worked it with his tongue until it hardened and he could feel Skye fighting to catch her breath. She leaned back against the bale of straw behind her and the motion lifted her breasts slightly, and Chase suckled her slowly while caressing the other hardening nipple with his thumb.

He reached down and took the kittens from her lap, placing them gently in the nest Desdemona had built between two nearby bales. Then he tugged Skye's shirt the rest of the way out of her jeans and spread it wide open, running his hands around her slender waist, up her back.

He drew his tongue slowly along the lacy trim of her bra, delving into the salty cleft between, and only then did she move, putting her hands on his shoulders as she let her head fall back with a soft moan.

He paused for half a heartbeat with his fingers on the front clasp of her bra, knowing there would be no turning back past this point. And then released it. Her breasts slipped free of their silken restraint and filled his hands and Skye drew in a sharp little breath and arched her back, offering herself to him, and in that instant Chase's self-control nearly broke.

He wanted her naked, damn it—naked and wrapped around him as tightly as a woman could get. Wanted her moaning his name as he sheathed himself in her, wanted to feel her trembling and bucking beneath him, wanted to feel the silken friction of skin on skin as he moved in those fierce, age-old rhythms of lovemaking.

Growling her name, he swung up onto his knees and grasped her around the waist with both hands to ease her gently around and down, pausing long enough to slip her out of her shirt and bra and tug her running shoes off. Then he unzipped her jeans and pulled them over her hips and thighs impatiently and tossed them aside, then even more impatiently eased her out of her silky blue briefs. And only then did he rock back onto his heels and gaze down at her, drinking in the perfection of her slim, naked body.

It was like being brushed with fire, Skye thought dizzily as Chase's hot, intense gaze moved over her hungrily. She could feel her breasts respond to the promise in that look, knew in some dim, half-aware way that this was exactly as it should be with this man, fast and urgent and without so much as a word spoken between them.

She had no idea what was happening, had never experienced anything even close to it in her entire life, knew it was dangerous and reckless and completely insane—and yet knew it was as right as life itself. Her body was aflame, and as Chase's gaze swept over her again she moaned faintly and arched her back, loving the things she was seeing in his eyes and knowing that it was her—looking at her, wanting her—that had put them there.

His eyes were narrowed and glittering and he grasped her ankles very gently and drew them apart, opening her for him, and Skye couldn't bite back the soft moan that broke from her throat, feeling more vulnerable than she ever had in her life before and yet unable to turn away.

He stretched out along her body, supporting himself on his outstretched arms, and lowered his mouth to hers. "You're not taking anything, are you?"

It took her a befuddled moment to realize what he was talking about, and when she finally did she shook her head, swallowing. "It—it doesn't matter. I don't care...."

"Shh." He kissed her again, less gently now, and then he eased himself backward and down, supporting her thighs with his forearms and lifting her knees slightly, and it was only when he dipped his head and kissed her more intimately than she'd ever imagined possible did she realize what he intended to do.

She gave a gasp of shock and tried to press her thighs together, but Chase slid his hands under her hips and held her firmly and in the next instant Skye's sharp little cry of surprise echoed through the loft.

"Chase? Chase McConnell, are you up there? If you are, you'd better get down here, and I mean now!"

Annie's voice cracked around Chase's ears like the snap of a bullwhip, and he recoiled so sharply he nearly saw stars, feeling guilty for things he hadn't even thought of yet. "Good God Almighty!" he whispered between clenched teeth.

Skye jackknifed into a sitting position, her face white with shock and then, a second later, turning a fiery crimson. She started snatching up her clothing and pulling it on, her hands trembling so badly she could scarcely fasten the hook on her bra.

"Chase!" Annie's voice snapped up from below.

"I'll be right down." There were a thousand things he should be saying to Skye, Chase thought a little remotely: comforting things, reassuring things. The things a man says to a woman he's almost made love to. Still wants to make love to...

The guilt was like something rank inside him, gnawing at him. Guilt at having taken it this far, at letting her believe that perhaps they had a future together when they didn't, guilt at wanting her, guilt at being here with her at all. He was still *married* to Joanne, damn it! He was widowed, not divorced.

"Phil Duggan is here with some papers he wants you to sign."

"I said I'll be right down!"

There was a mutter, then the sound of Annie's footsteps crossing the barn and he heard the hinges on the door squeal open, then close again. He sat there for a moment longer, then swore savagely at nothing at all and lunged to his feet, reaching for his hat. "Are you all right?" he asked Skye roughly.

"I'm fine."

She sounded anything but fine, he thought. She sounded shaken up and scared and as confused as he was.

"Don't wait for me. I—I'll be down in a while."

"All right." He turned to leave, then found himself glancing around at her again. She was pulling on her running shoes, fumbling with the laces ineffectually, and he wondered idly if she was crying. He still had the taste of her in his mouth, warm and a little salty, still wanted her so badly he was dizzy with it. And he found himself wondering idly, standing there watching her, if he wouldn't be smarter just to make love to her and get it over with.

A car horn sounded just then, loud and impatient, and he swore in frustration, torn between staying and going. Knowing, even as he stood there, that he had no choice. And finally he just wheeled away and headed for the ladder. "See you later."

* * *

The sun was starting to go down by the time Skye finally descended from the loft, stiff and a little cold, and walked back to the house.

A car was parked in the driveway, a luxury late-model Detroit product, fully loaded, and she looked at it with a sinking heart. Facing Chase after what had happened was going to be bad enough without having to play the role of loving wife on top of it. She could swear that all anyone had to do was look at her to know exactly what she'd been doing—it must be written all over her!

Just thinking about it made her cheeks burn again. What in heaven's name had she been thinking of, letting it go that far? Chase must think . . . well, God knows what Chase thought. He'd been abrupt and cool afterward, almost angry. As disgusted with himself as with her, probably. The *last* thing he needed in his life right now were any more complications.

Not that she needed any in *hers* either, she reminded herself. This was all just pretend, damn it. Forget that for even a moment—fall in love even a little—and she was going to be sorry.

Taking a deep breath, she walked into the house.

The big living room was dim enough that someone—Annie, probably—had turned on some of the table lamps, and it glowed with warmth and a welcoming friendliness, as a comfortable home should. There was a fire snapping on the hearth, too, and the sound of a child's laughter, and for a moment—just a heartbeat, actually—Skye felt a jab of wistfulness that it wasn't real.

There was a man seated on one of the big sofas bracketing the stone fireplace. His thick silver hair was expensively styled, his suede Western-cut blazer and camel slacks, like the tooled leather boots, custom-made, and he gave off that aura of money and power that some men seem born with.

Sarah was sitting beside him with a book in her lap and she looked up, and broke into a huge smile when she saw Skye.

"You're back!" She wriggled off the sofa and took two or three twisted, painful steps toward Skye, grinning. "I thought you and Dad were off riding or something. I told Grandpa you'd be back if he just waited awhile."

"Sorry, honey." Skye's heart gave a thud as she knelt to give Sarah a hug, trying to keep her expression blank. So this was Tup Hewitt! "I...ummm...just lost track of time. You were having a nap when I left." So Chase wasn't here. Had he gone into town on business? Or just hadn't wanted to face her?

Hewitt eased himself to his feet, rising a solid six feet in the firelight, his expression as bland as Skye's. He extended his hand and smiled down at her graciously. "Tup Hewitt."

"This is Skye," Sarah piped up proudly.

His eyes were a piercing blue, and Skye felt them go right through her, assessing and weighing, and she wondered what he thought of her, the woman who had taken his beloved daughter's place in Chase's life.

Found herself wishing, too, that she'd come in the back way and had slipped upstairs to change and comb some of the straw out of her hair. He seemed to be taking that in, as well, undoubtedly wondering what she'd been up to.

"I'm delighted to finally meet you, Mr. Hewitt. Chase has mentioned you often."

"I'll bet he has." Those sharp blue eyes met hers head-on.

But Skye held them evenly, smiling. "I'm sorry he's not here, but he'll be in soon. In the meantime, I'd like some coffee—how about you?"

"I got a cup when I came in, but I wouldn't mind another one." His gaze flickered over her curiously. "And I didn't come to see my son-in-law, Mrs. McConnell. I came to see you."

"How nice." Skye smiled with feigned delight, wondering how long she was going to be able to play the loving mother and doting wife. This man was no one's fool. One false step, one wrong word, and she'd bring the whole thing crashing down around their heads. "And please, call me 'Skye.' If you'll excuse me for a moment . . . ?"

Annie was in the kitchen, cutting up a chicken at the island center, and she gave Skye's tousled hair and clothing a disapproving look, then pointedly ignored her.

"Annie, will you please bring coffee and some of that maple cake in for Mr. Hewitt and myself? And a glass of milk for Sarah."

"Tup Hewitt doesn't like maple cake," Annie said flatly.

Taking a deep breath, Skye walked the few steps it took to face Annie directly across the counter. "You listen to me," she said in a quiet, tight voice. "If that man in there has his way, he's going to prove that Chase can't care for Sarah and is going to take her away. And I don't need to tell you what that will do to Chase. So unless you want *that* on your conscience, you'll help me convince Tup Hewitt that we're all one happy little family out here, do you understand me?"

"You're not married to him at all, are you?" Annie's eyes were defiant.

Skye stared at the other woman for a long moment. Then, finally, she let her shoulders drop in defeat, tired of the lies and the pretending. "No. We hoped that being married would help prove Chase is able to take care of Sarah properly."

"He could have told me. I wouldn't have given it away, you know. He should have known he could trust *me*, of all people!"

"It was wrong to lie to you, Annie, but Chase was trying to protect you. If this thing falls apart, and it could very easily, he didn't want you taking any of the blame."

Annie gave a sniff. "I knew it all along! I've got eyes. And you two didn't act like any newlyweds I've ever seen." Her eyes narrowed suddenly. "But you're sleeping in the same bed."

Skye managed a rough smile and shook her head. "Chase sleeps on the floor. We mess the bed up in the morning to make it look like we slept together, but he's never... we're not..."

Not quite, she thought unsteadily, refusing to think about what had *almost* happened in the loft.

"Well, if that don't beat all." Annie gave her graying head a shake. "You'd better get back in there and do what you have to do. I'll bring in coffee and pie—Mr. Hewitt does like my apple pie. And it seems to me," she added with a sharp look at Skye, "that you've earned yourself a piece, too."

It was, Skye realized, the closest thing she was going to get to a vote of support, and she managed another smile. "Thanks, Annie."

"It's too bad in a way."

Skye, halfway to the dining room door, paused and looked around questioningly.

Annie smiled. "Too bad it isn't real. He needs a woman again. It's time he was done with the grieving and got on. Sarah don't just need a mother, she needs a father, too. Chase spends too much time with his memories for it to be healthy for either of them." The smile widened almost mischievously. "He's right taken with you—it's written all over his face every time he looks at you. Is there any chance...?"

"None at all," Skye replied evenly. "I'm sorry."

Skye set her mouth into a welcoming smile as she walked back into the living room. "Is Mrs. Hewitt with you?"

"Barbara was tied up with a fund-raiser dinner." Tup's shrewd gaze met hers. "She's looking forward to meeting you. Chase's marriage came as quite a...surprise."

"Yes, I know." Skye gave him her very warmest smile. "It was quite a surprise to us, too. Chase just popped the question, and I said yes before either of us knew what had hit us."

"Is that so." He nodded slowly, his gaze holding hers as though hoping to catch her in a lie. "Sarah tells me you're a teacher."

"Yes." Carefully Skye contemplated the question, trying to anticipate where she might trip herself up.

"And do you plan to teach here this fall?"

"I...don't know. I haven't checked into the teaching situation here at all yet. I'd like to spend as much time with Sarah as possible." Which wasn't, really, a lie at all.

"She says you're helping her with her reading. Seem to be doing a pretty good job, too—she was showing off her skills." He smiled down at his granddaughter and touched her head lovingly, and Skye felt her heart turn over. One thing was certain—this man adored the little girl smiling at his side. If he was trying to take her away from Chase, part of it, at least, was sincere concern for his granddaughter.

Damn. It would have been easier, Skye thought irritably, if the man had turned out to be a monster. As least then the sides would have been clearly marked, the lines clearly drawn between good and evil.

"You'll excuse me for saying this, Mrs. McConnell, but—"

"'Skye.'" She looked at him evenly for a moment, then decided to risk a frontal attack. Tup Hewitt was not the kind of man to appreciate subterfuge. "Please, I'd like to say something."

He didn't reply, just stood there looking at her with a cool expression, and Skye braced herself. "I know this is awkward for you, Mr. Hewitt. It's awkward for me, too. Chase loved your daughter very much, and I know it's hard for you to come into this house and see me where she should be. But I hope you won't hate me for that. I'm not trying to take your daughter's place."

"I know that," he said gruffly, frowning as he sat down. He caressed Sarah's head absently as the little girl leaned against the arm of the sofa, his expression pensive. And oddly vulnerable. "I appreciate your candor, young woman. It's a damn rare trait these days, and I admire it. Joanne was the same way—the way I taught her."

"She must have been a wonderful person," Skye said truthfully. "I think I would have liked her."

"Everyone liked Joanne." He smiled fondly at Sarah. "Your mother was my... my life. When she died, a little of me died, too."

"Daddy doesn't like us to talk about her," Sarah said uncomfortably.

"Your father—" Tup caught himself. "Honey, how about going in to see how that coffee's coming along? Can you do that?"

"Of course I can," Sarah replied with a hint of long-suffering tolerance in her voice. "Honestly, I'm not a *cripple*."

Tup's grin was rueful, but his expression was riven with pain as he watched Sarah make her slow and awkward way from the room. "It breaks my heart to see her like that. I wanted to take her to New York, to a specialist there, but Chase wouldn't hear of it."

"The orthopedic team in Portland is one of the best in the country," Skye said carefully, trying not to push. "And I suspect Sarah would benefit more from being close to home. And Chase."

Tup's smile was speculative. "You're not afraid of me, are you?"

"Should I be?"

"Most people are." He chuckled. "I like it that way, to be honest. But it's refreshing to meet someone with a little old-fashioned courage. Keeps me humble."

"I was raised by people who believed in free speech, Mr. Hewitt. I was born during a civil rights demonstration in Alabama, and grew up surrounded by people ready to die for their beliefs. Some of them did. I was taught not to be afraid to speak out when I see something I disagree with."

It was a risk, she knew that, and she held her breath . . . and eased it out when Tup's steely blue eyes flickered with honest amusement. "I like you, young lady. I'll say one thing for Chase McConnell—he's got one hell of an eye for a good woman."

And Skye, blushing slightly, had to laugh. "Thank you."

"I suppose you know I'm thinking about trying to get Sarah's grandmother and myself declared her legal guardians."

"Chase mentioned something about it. I'd hoped he was wrong, Mr. Hewitt. You won't find a more loving father anywhere."

"I'm not saying Chase isn't a good father. But the boy's almost bankrupt. Hell, it'll take twenty years of hard labor to get this place out from under the mortgages he's got on it. And Sarah's got another two, maybe three operations yet, plus all the other expenses. He just doesn't have the money to provide her the care she needs—it's that simple. Love can't do it all.''

"Love can do just about anything," Skye said softly. "There must be another way. You can't take Sarah away from him."

"The way he took Joanne away from me?" The words were bitter, and they filled the room with old pain. "My daughter would be alive today if he hadn't married Chase McConnell. His pride killed her. If he'd let me give her that new car for her birthday, she wouldn't have been driving that broken-down old truck . . . and she'd be alive today."

"I told you to stay the hell out of my house, Hewitt."

The cold, angry voice came from the shadows somewhere behind her, and Skye started slightly. She glanced around just as Chase strode into the center of the room, large and almost menacing in the firelight, his face like stone.

Seven

"I wasn't planning on staying." The two men faced each other across the living room, the animosity between them almost giving off sparks. "I just came to see my granddaughter."

"Daddy!" Sarah appeared in the dining room just then, and her face literally lit up the room when she saw Chase. She hurried toward him as best she could, nearly falling when her twisted foot caught on the edge of the rug.

It was Hewitt who got to her first, steadying her as she grabbed for the back of a chair to catch her balance, her cane hitting the hardwood floor with a crack that made Chase flinch. Seemingly unperturbed by her near fall, she just grinned at them and continued across to her father.

"Damn it, sweetheart, I wish you'd be careful."

Chase's face was the color of old bone, and Skye could see the deep lines around his mouth, and the anguish in his eyes as he hunkered down onto his heels and returned Sarah's hug.

"Oh, Dad." Sarah rolled her eyes. "I fall all the time, but I don't hurt myself." Her eyes widened. "Did you see the Sarahmobile that Granddad brought me? It's got independent suspension so it won't tip over, and a motor with three speeds and a roll bar and—"

"A *what?*" Chase stood up slowly, looking at Tup.

"It's a small all-terrain vehicle," Hewitt said mildly. "I had the shop modify it so Sarah can use it easily. Top speed's about five miles an hour, so she won't be breaking any records. But it'll give her more mobility and take her places she can't go now."

"I told you I didn't want you buying her things." Chase's voice vibrated with fury. "She doesn't need your expensive toys, Hewitt. I can take her anywhere she wants to go. Quit trying to buy her off!"

"Dad, Granddad just—"

"Take it back, Hewitt. I don't want it on the Rocking M."

"Daddy!"

"Damn it, McConnell, stop being so—"

"Stop it!" Skye's voice snapped through the room so sharply that all three of them turned their heads to stare at her in surprise. She strode across to where the two men were facing each other and gave Chase an angry look of warning. Then, smiling warmly, she turned to Tup. "It's a wonderful gift, Mr. Hewitt. Sarah's going to get a lot of enjoyment out of it."

"No way," Chase grated. "That thing goes with him."

"I don't think so, *darling.*" Stressing the one word just enough to make Chase look at her, she smiled up at him sweetly and slipped her arm through his, leaning against him like the loving wife she was supposed to be. "I think it's a fabulous idea! Sarah will be able to get down to the stable by herself and—"

"And down to the pond to visit Hamlet," Sarah piped up. "And Granddad said they designed it special so it'll go through doors, so I can help Annie set the table again and carry stuff and everything!"

"Damn it, *darling*...." Chase's voice was tight and his eyes were practically giving off sparks.

Skye just smiled. And, under cover of her own body so Hewitt couldn't see, she fastened her thumb and forefinger on the tender flesh on the inside of Chase's elbow and pinched...hard. "You do agree, don't you...? Sweetheart?"

"She can try it out." Chase got out from between gritted teeth, his eyes smoldering. He tried to slip his arm free of Skye's, but she held it firmly.

"Good." Hewitt smiled, then bent down to kiss Sarah and give her a hug. Then he nodded to Skye, his eyes filled with amusement and speculation and about six dozen other things she didn't even try to interpret.

"Tell Annie I'm sorry I couldn't stay for coffee. And I'm very glad to have met you, young lady. Very glad, indeed." And with that, he turned and strode across the living room and out of the house.

"Just what the *hell* did you—"

"Later, darling," Skye murmured to Chase very agreeably, her smile so sweet it hurt her mouth. "I don't think this is the time to discuss this."

Chase's nostrils flared and the look he gave her could have melted tempered steel. But he did manage to restrain himself, muttering something about halter breaking and hog tying that Skye didn't catch in its entirety. Probably, she decided by the expression on his face, for the better.

To Skye's relief, Annie came sailing in just then with a huge tray laden with a silver coffeepot and cups and cutlery and plates of apple pie. She looked around the room in surprise, then took a second, closer, look at Chase. Eyes darkening, she walked across and set the tray down on the coffee table with a bang.

"Guess you can serve yourselves, since the young Lord ran the company off."

Chase started to draw in a deep breath, but Skye stepped between them. "Thanks, Annie. Maybe you could take Sarah's milk and a slice of that pie outside to the picnic table—she can show you the new Sarahmobile."

"But don't you guys want to see it?" Sarah asked in concern.

"Yes, honey, but first your father and I have something to talk about. We'll be out in a little while, all right?"

"Oh-oh." Sarah's smile was mischievous. "You're going to get it now, Daddy!" She turned and looked at Annie. "We'd better go. They're going to have a big fight and don't want me to hear."

"Seems to me it's about time some things got said around here." Annie glared across at Chase. "Isn't *my* place, or I'd have said 'em a long time ago."

"I've never seen you short on opinions," Chase growled. "And I've got things to—"

"Later." Skye used her best schoolteacher voice. It startled Chase so badly he stopped in midstride and looked around at her in alarm.

Then he whispered something under his breath and nodded abruptly, narrowed eyes glittering. Walking across to the fireplace, he braced one arm on the mantel and stared down into the flames, his face set and hard.

As she heard the outside door bang closed behind Annie and Sarah, Skye drew in a deep breath, bracing herself.

She didn't have long to wait. Chase wheeled toward her before the sound of the closing door had even died away, vibrant with anger. ''Just what the hell do you think you're doing?''

''Keeping you from making one of the biggest mistakes of your life!''

''Lady, this is none of your business!''

''Oh, yes it is. You *made* it my business the minute you brought me through that front door and dumped me in the middle of this mess!''

''I don't want him coming in here tossing money at her like there's no tomorrow. He's just trying to buy her away from me, for crying out loud!''

''If that's so, then I feel even sorrier for him than I do for you. But you're walking right into it, Chase. Every time he gives something to Sarah and you take it away, *you're* the heavy.'' She caught most of her anger, lowering her voice with an effort.

''Of course it galls you that he can afford to buy her all the things you can't. That's a natural reaction any father would have. But sometimes—when it's in Sarah's best interests—you'd be a lot smarter to swallow your pride and let him play the benevolent, rich grandfather. It's not going to make you *less* of a father.''

''He used to do the same thing with Joanne,'' he said heatedly, starting to pace. ''He was always buying her expensive gifts...clothes, horses, jewelry. All the things I couldn't afford to give her.''

''And it hurt your pride.''

''A husband is supposed to be able to provide for his wife,'' he muttered sullenly.

"I suspect you did," Skye said almost absently, watching the firelight play on his strong features with a touch of envy for the woman who had not just this man, but his love. "She was very lucky. . . ." Then she shook it off. "If you continue to compete with Tup Hewitt for Sarah's love, you're going to lose her, Chase."

He stared down at her for a long, silent while. "What makes you give a damn, anyway? Especially after—" He cut his words off.

Because in spite of all my best intentions I'm falling in love with you and Sarah and the Rocking M and everything all of you have to offer, she found herself thinking a little inanely.

She let her gaze drop from his, afraid he might see some of this in her eyes, and shrugged as carelessly as she could manage. "Just a soft touch, I guess. I won't buy tuna because of the dolphins, I won't use products from companies that do lab tests on animals and I put on bottle drives to collect money to save the rain forests. Give me a cause, and I jump right in."

His gaze moved across her face almost curiously, then, impossibly, a ghost of a smile flickered across his mouth, gone in a heartbeat. "You know, Red, if things were different . . ."

"But they're not, McConnell." Skye managed a casual smile. "Let's not start making promises we can't keep, all right?"

"This afternoon . . ." He frowned, looking perplexed and a little uneasy. "I didn't mean to scare you."

"You didn't," she lied.

"Oh?" Again that ghost smile crossed his mouth. "I managed to scare myself pretty bad. Anyway, I just thought I should tell you it won't happen again."

"That's probably just as well."

"Yeah." He nodded, almost wearily, and turned away. "Yeah, that's the way I figure it, too."

He went out not long after supper, and didn't come back until nearly midnight, well after Skye was in bed. She pretended to be asleep as he moved quietly around the room, and tried to concentrate on keeping her breathing slow and even and not on the unnervingly erotic fantasies that kept filling her mind.

He turned the light out finally and she lay in the moonlight and listened to him stirring restlessly in his makeshift bed.

Neither of them slept much. She'd doze off now and again, only to awaken a few minutes later, heart pounding. Chase was up and down two or three times, prowling the shadowed room while she lay motionless, watching him through half-slitted eyes and pretending to be asleep.

He'd wander for a while, then swear under his breath and crawl back into his rough bed. She'd listen to the sound of his breathing in the darkness, knowing he was as wide-awake as she, listening to her, every breath, every swallow, every movement magnified. Knowing if she turned her head she'd find him looking at her. And knowing what she'd see in his eyes if she did.

The tension built until it hummed through the room like a wind blowing over harp strings, a vibrant man-woman thing so vital and uncomplicatedly sexual that she lay there barely breathing, half-terrified he was going to ease himself to his feet and come to her. Equally terrified that she'd welcome him if he did.

Finally, just before dawn, she drifted into an uneasy sleep and dreamed a confusing, erotic dream in which she opened her eyes and saw him standing by the bed and lifted the sheet for him, and he slipped into her arms. As he started making love to her, she awakened with a jolt, her body aching with a need that made her turn her face into her pillow and weep silently, wishing she knew what was happening to her. Part of her knowing, and not wanting to. . . .

In the morning, he was gone. The comforter was draped across the foot of the bed and his pillow lay beside hers, still indented by the weight of his head. She could have sworn it was still warm, and she put her hand out and touched it, catching a hint of the clean scent of his skin and hair, and was filled with a sudden aching emptiness that made her squeeze her eyes closed against a welling of tears.

The next couple of days were strange ones, as far as Chase was concerned. For one thing, he was seeing a hell of a lot more of Skye than he knew was a good idea, but for the life of him he couldn't stay away from her.

Sometimes it was almost accidental, as when he'd forget something and had to go back up to the bedroom in the morning just as she'd be getting out of the shower. She'd come out of the bathroom wrapped in a terry-cloth robe and scented steam, with tendrils of wet hair clinging to her throat and shoulders. The two of them would move around the room self-consciously, talking about nothing at all while she gathered up lacy under things, and he'd try not to think of dragging her gently into the big, unmade bed and making love to her as though his very life depended on it.

And at other times it would be deliberate. He'd find himself wandering through the big empty house until he found her, and he'd stand looking at her while she did whatever it was she was doing—helping Annie in the kitchen, weeding the rose beds out front, playing with Sarah—until he'd had his fill. Then he'd go back to what-

ever he'd been doing until the need to see her got too strong
to ignore and he'd go through the entire routine again and
again and again....

Part of it, he was certain, was just sex.

It was on his mind a lot lately. In teeth-grinding, erotic
detail. It wouldn't take much—a hint of perfume on the
still air, the way Skye would hold the tip of her tongue
against her upper lip when she was concentrating on
something, a glimpse of her in those faded old jeans that
cupped her taut little bottom the way he dreamed of doing. The curve of a shoulder, the play of sunlight on her
hair... hell, all it took was one of a thousand little things
and he'd practically be pawing the dirt.

But part of it was just... Skye. The way she tipped her
head to one side when she laughed. The gentleness in her
eyes when she looked at Sarah. The faint blush that would
caress her cheeks when she caught him looking at her. Just
being around her. Knowing she was there. Things that
shouldn't have mattered, that didn't make any sense.

But the part he liked best, aside from waking in the night
and listening to her soft breathing as she slept, was the af-
ter-supper ritual they'd started after Tup had brought what
everyone called the Sarahmobile.

It was, he had to grudgingly admit, a work of engineer-
ing genius. A cross between an electric wheelchair and a
golf cart, it had a sturdy fiberglass body that sat low on
four fat wheels, making it all but impossible to tip over,
although a roll bar had been added just as an extra safety
feature. It was outfitted with hand rails so Sarah could pull
herself into the driver's seat without assistance, and a
heavy vinyl canopy that could be pulled up to protect the
driver. And, to make it easier for her, the throttle and
brake were controlled from a handlebar apparatus that
Chase suspected had started life on a motorcycle.

Chase's fears that Sarah would promptly kill herself on it had proved baseless. It puttered along at a top speed of about five miles an hour and was little threat to either Sarah or anything that might get in her way, but that didn't seem to lessen Sarah's delight with it. It had taken her about five minutes to become an expert on it, and she was all over the ranch now, scaring the cattle and stampeding the occasional horse and just generally raising hell the way she once had.

And although he'd never gotten around to it yet, Chase knew he was going to have to thank Skye for insisting that he let her keep it.

As a matter of fact, he mused lazily, he was going to have to thank her for a number of things one of these days. And helping put the healthy glow back in Sarah's cheeks was only one of them. She'd managed to put a bit of a glow back into his own while she'd been at it, and there were whole days that would go by now when he wouldn't have to consciously fight the emptiness and the despair.

He glanced down at her, liking the way she looked striding along beside him, that firecracker head of hair nearly giving off sparks in the setting sun. They hadn't said much on the walk down to the pond, but they rarely did, the silence between them friendly and comfortable, and he let himself just relax into it.

They'd picked up quite an entourage this evening, including old Jack, who seemed to enjoy the evening walk as much as Chase did, and a gray-and-white Persian called Juliet, who strolled just ahead of them like a queen leading her royal procession, her parade-banner tail wafting gently as the five of them meandered companionably through the lowering sun.

Sarah would put on a burst of speed and get ahead of them, then would stop and wait for Skye and Chase to catch up, glowing with mischief and fresh air and energy. And as they started back to the house, Chase draped his arm casually across Skye's shoulders as though it was the most normal thing in the world.

It was strange, he mused, how he caught himself now and again thinking it was real—that Skye and he really *were* married. It was hard to believe she'd only been here a handful of days—seven, maybe—and that in another seven or eight she'd be gone and in all likelihood he'd never see her again.

"And it's just so beautiful, I hate to think of it being turned into a resort."

Caught with his mind wandering, Chase looked down at Skye questioningly. She was gazing across the valley at the heavily forested bulk of Mary's Mountain where it sat outlined against the rose-and-azure sky. They came to a stop, and Skye seemed to lean against him slightly.

"Who *was* Mary, anyway?"

"My great-grandmother, Mary Margaret Finnerty."

"And how did Mary Margaret Finnerty manage to have an entire mountain named after her?"

"Damned if I know. The old homestead is still up there. And a small family cemetery. Mary and my great grand-dad, Brian McConnell, are buried up there."

"But...my God!" Skye looked up at him with a shocked expression. "You can't possibly sell that land!"

Chase stared up at the dark profile of the mountain, feeling something rip away inside him just at the thought of losing it. "I don't have any choice, Skye. Sentiment is great, but it won't pay Sarah's medical bills."

"But this is..." She sputtered for a moment, gesturing angrily. "This is outrageous! A man shouldn't have to sell his great-grandparent's *graves* to pay medical bills, for heaven's sake! That's not just a piece of property—it's a piece of history. A piece of what being a McConnell is all about!''

Chase smiled humorlessly. "Try that line on the next bunch of bills that comes in and see how far it gets you, Red.''

"No." She shook her head firmly, her eyes flashing in the shadowed light. "There's got to be some other way. There is *always* another way. We'll write to the governor. We'll—''

"No." Chase's voice was harsher than he'd intended, and he stared across at the mountain. "The sale's going to be finalized in another couple of weeks and that will be the end of it. You can't hang on to things forever. Sarah's what counts here, not a hunk of real estate, regardless of its past.''

Skye drew in a breath as though to say something, then subsided, looking up at him thoughtfully. Then she just nodded and they started walking again, and after a moment or two Chase reached out and pulled her close to him, wanting, for just that little while, to pretend that she was real.

"You and Daddy aren't really married, are you?" Sarah, chin planted firmly in her cupped palms, gazed at Skye curiously.

They'd been eating a midmorning snack of ice cream out at the picnic table in the backyard, talking about nothing very much until then. The question caught Skye so unexpectedly that she blinked, her mind wheeling as she struggled to come up with an answer. "I...um...that is, we...in the true *spirit* of marriage, Sarah, we..." She gave up.

"You're just pretending to be married so Granddad Hewitt won't take me away from Daddy."

Skye took a deep breath. "How did you find out?"

"I just figured it out."

Terrific, Skye thought. So much for Chase's theory that their pretend marriage was going to fool the court officials that Hewitt had investigating him—it wasn't even fooling a seven-year-old!

"I just wish you *were* married," Sarah said wistfully. "I wish it were real. I really like having you for a mom."

"Oh, Sarah..." Skye slipped her arms around Sarah's slender shoulders and hugged her tightly. "If there were some way I could make it real, I would. I'm going to miss you so much...."

"But you're not leaving, are you?" Sarah's voice rose with alarm.

"Not right away, but I can't stay." Skye drew back, brushing a strand of silver-gold hair from the child's anxious face. "Honey, it was wrong to lie to you. Your dad was desperate and we came up with this crazy idea without even thinking it through properly. We never meant to hurt you."

"I'm going to tell Dad that he should marry you for real," Sarah muttered. "Then Granddad Hewitt won't try to take me to live with him and Grandma." She looked up at Skye. "I like Granddad and Grandma Hewitt and I have lots of fun when I'm there. But I don't want to *live* with them! I want to live with my dad."

"Well, if everything works out, you'll be staying right here," Skye told her reassuringly. And if it doesn't? If Hewitt convinces the courts that Sarah would be better off with him and his wife...what are you going to tell her then?

Except you won't be here to tell her anything, part of her taunted. You'll be back in Portland. It'll be easy for you— you won't have to break the news to her or watch her father rage against an uncaring universe . . . it won't concern you at all.

Skye smiled grimly. If she could only believe that! She'd be carrying these people—and their pain—around with her for years.

She reached out and wiped a smear of ice cream from Sarah's chin. "Let's clean these dishes up, then go for a walk."

Sarah brightened a little. "We could go up to Yellow Rock Canyon and see the Indian petroglyphs."

"It's pretty hot," Skye said doubtfully. "I was thinking more of going down to the pond and dabbling our feet in the water."

"You should have brought a sundress." Sarah eyed Skye's T-shirt and jeans. "Didn't you even bring any shorts?"

"Nope. I was on my way to visit an old friend when your dad...talked me into helping him. Carly and I had planned to shop for new summer clothes, so I hardly brought anything with me."

"I . . . ummm . . . know where you can find a sundress. And I bet it would fit and everything."

"Not one of Annie's?"

Sarah giggled. "No! There's a box of stuff in the spare bedroom. It belonged to . . . Emma."

"Emma?" Skye started gathering up the dishes. "Who's Emma?"

"She...stayed with us for a little while. Last year. Right after I had my first operation."

"A nurse?"

"Sort of. She was a friend of Dad's."

"Oh." It was ridiculous, Skye thought, but for half an instant she'd actually felt . . . jealous. "A . . . uh . . . girlfriend?"

"Sort of. But it wasn't anything *serious*. I mean, you could still wear her clothes."

"Why did she leave them behind?"

"She . . . she got married. She told Dad to mail her stuff to her, but then I guess she forgot to tell him the address or something. She's in France now. They make wine."

"Sounds as though Emma's done pretty well for herself," Skye muttered, wondering if the faint resentment she felt was at the woman's successful marriage, or the fact that she'd been a close friend of Chase's. "Let's shove this stuff into the dishwasher, then we'll see if Emma left anything behind that will fit me."

The box was pushed into the depths of the closet in one of the spare bedrooms, and by the time Skye got it wrestled into the open she was hot and tousled and having second thoughts.

"I'm not sure about this," she said doubtfully as Sarah started rummaging through it happily. "It doesn't seem right somehow. She left an awful lot of stuff behind."

"Oh, it's okay." Sarah smiled up at Skye beatifically. "Emma wouldn't mind. There's a pretty sundress in here..." She started rummaging energetically again. "Here it is!"

When she took the folded garment and shook it out, Skye felt some of her doubts crumble. Even badly wrinkled, the dress was every bit as pretty as Sarah had promised. It was white, with an apple green floral design appliquéd across the front, and Skye had to admit that it looked cool and comfortable. Thought, idly, of what Chase might think if he saw her in it. . . .

"Oh, heck," she breathed, holding the dress up to herself and giving a pirouette. "I guess it can't do any harm. I'll wear it while I'm here, then wash it and pack it away, and with luck, Emma will be none the wiser."

Annie had the ironing board already set up in the laundry room, so it didn't take Skye more than a few minutes to have the dress pressed and looking like new. Back in the spare room where she'd left Sarah rooting through the box and its treasures, she slipped out of her jeans, T-shirt and bra, and into the sundress.

"Mmm. Not bad." Skye gave the bodice a tug. It was a little loose, but aside from that, the dress fitted perfectly. Turning this way and that, she nodded with approval. "Okay. Now how about that walk?"

"Do you want to see something?" Sarah looked up at her shyly.

"Sure. What have you got?"

"It belonged to my mom." Sarah held out the golden locket reverently. "Annie gave it to me a long time ago, but I had to promise not to tell anyone."

Skye cupped the locket in her palm. "It's beautiful, Sarah. Why don't you ever wear it? I think your mom would like that."

"Dad would get real mad if he even knew I had it," Sarah whispered. "He doesn't like anyone talking about her. And he gets real upset if he sees anything that belonged to her."

Skye nodded sadly, turning the locket in her fingers. It snapped open and she found herself gazing at a tiny photograph of an attractive blonde-haired woman with wide, blue eyes and a smile that lit up the entire room. But it was the photo in the other half of the locket that made Skye's heart give a twist, the gray-eyed cowboy who was grinning into the camera in that reckless, lazy way she knew so well, his gaze seeming to capture hers and hold it.

Seeing them like that, together, so happy and so obviously in love, hurt more than she could have imagined. She snapped the locket closed abruptly, her eyes smarting.

What was wrong with her? You'd think she was in love with Chase McConnell herself, the way she was behaving lately!

"There's some pictures here, too." Sarah had the carton half unpacked by now, and was rooting through the bottom third like a mouse in a bran bin, elbows flying.

And Skye, watching her, had a sudden and very unpleasant premonition. "Sarah...."

"Yeah?" She popped her head out of the box, grinning. "Found them! And there's this neat box with all sorts of—"

"Sarah, Emma never existed at all, did she? These are your mother's things."

Sarah let her gaze slip away from Skye's, her cheeks turning pink. She gazed down at the envelope in her hands, picking at the torn flap. "I knew if I told you it was Mom's stuff, you wouldn't let me look at it."

"Sarah, it wasn't right to lie to me like that." Skye had to fight a smile. "Living in France, making wine! Honestly!"

"Well, you lied to me." Sarah gave an uncomfortable wriggle.

Skye nodded unhappily. "I know. And it's hypocritical of me to tell you how wrong it is—but lying is *never* an answer."

"I know," Sarah whispered in a tiny voice. "But I couldn't pull the box out by myself, not since the accident. And it's been such a long time since I've been able to look."

"You mean you've been through these things before?"

Sarah looked at her pleadingly. "Don't tell Annie, please? She doesn't know I even know it's here. I used to sit in here all the time before my accident and look at the pictures and stuff." The wide blue eyes filled with tears suddenly. "This is all I have left, Skye. Daddy won't talk about her, and Annie tries sometimes, and then she starts crying. I hardly remember her anymore. It's not as though I'm doing something bad, is it? It doesn't feel bad. It's like she's here almost. Sometimes I even talk to her...." Her voice faltered and she ducked her head, giving her cheeks a swipe with her arm. "I just want to know her."

Skye had to swallow, hard, to keep her voice steady. "No, Sarah, you're not doing anything bad. Going against your dad isn't right, but I don't think he realizes how important this is to you."

"You won't tell, will you?" Sarah gazed up at her earnestly.

"I won't tell. But when the timing's right, you've got to tell him yourself."

Sarah nodded. "And you're not going to put this all away, are you? Not yet, I mean? Annie won't be back for hours, and Dad's way up on Mary's Mountain with the surveyors and it's too hot to go for a walk, anyway, isn't it?"

It was wrong, Skye thought. Wrong to go against Chase, wrong to encourage Sarah to defy her father's wishes. And yet, gazing down into Sarah's small tear-stained face, she found she didn't have the strength to say no. What harm could come of a child's need to know a mother she hardly remembered? And what right did anyone—even a grieving father—have to deny Sarah that bond of love she so desperately needed?

"Half an hour" she heard herself saying. "Then everything goes back in the box, and the box goes back in the closet."

"Can I at least keep a picture out? Grandma Hewitt gave me one last year, but Daddy found it and took it away."

She was probably going to live to regret this, Skye thought grimly. One did not meddle in the inner workings of family without winding up regretting it. "I guess it can't hurt if you keep one picture out," she said quietly. "But for heaven's sake, keep it hidden!" There. Now she wasn't just advising Sarah to defy her father, she was telling her to lie to him, as well. Great role model *you* are, she advised herself disgustedly.

But it didn't take her long to fall under the spell of Sarah's happiness. There were envelopes of loose photographs, some dating back to Joanne's childhood, and a small wooden box filled with letters—although Skye flatly drew the line at letting Sarah open any of them—and a couple of dried corsages, a gold cuff link, a tiny notebook filled with pressed flowers: the kind of silly mementos that mean nothing to anyone else, yet mean everything to the person who has kept them.

Skye stayed out of it, relaxing on the padded seat built into the bay window while Sarah looked and touched to her heart's content. The morning drew on lazily, filled with the drone of bees moving languidly in the honeysuckle outside the screened window and the occasional giggle or exclamation of delight from Sarah.

The heat made Skye drowsy and she had to fight to keep her eyes open, giving in finally and letting them slide closed and just drifting. . . .

It was the sound of booted footsteps in the corridor just outside the door that jarred her awake, and she looked around wildly, trying to figure out how long she'd been asleep. No more than a minute or two at the most . . . and yet long enough, she realized with a sense of horror. Long enough. . . .

The footsteps paused, then the door pushed in and Skye found herself staring into Chase McConnell's startled gray eyes.

Eight

For one tiny, impossible eye-blink of time, Chase actually thought it was Joanne sitting there in the bay window, wearing that sundress that always drove him a little crazy.

He grabbed the door frame, feeling disoriented and a little sick, knowing that it was just a bizarre dream.

But the expression of shock on Sarah's face was no dream. And the dawning horror on Skye's wasn't, either, as she slowly got to her feet, her face so white that her eyes looked like deep pools of green water.

"Chase, I—I can explain..."

"Dad, don't get mad at Skye. It was all my—"

"What the hell do you think you're doing?" Eyes riveted on Skye, he took two long strides into the room, his voice just a hoarse whisper, torn from him.

"Dad, it's just—"

"Get that dress off." He took another step toward Skye, having to fight to keep from reaching out and tearing it from her.

"Dad!"

Sarah was on her feet by then, and he looked down at her angrily. "I told you *never* to touch these things."

"But Daddy, we were only—"

"Get down to your room, Sarah. Now!"

She recoiled, looking stunned and hurt. Then her eyes filled and she turned and stumbled from the room, her sobs going through him like a knife blade. The slamming door made him flinch.

"She's seven years old, for heaven's sake!" Skye said angrily. "She's got a normal curiosity about her mother, and you're only making things worse if you—"

"Nobody asked you!" Chase turned on her savagely. "She never disobeyed me before you got here. You're only pretending to be her mother, not trying to take Joanne's place!"

"Joanne's dead!" Skye's voice ricocheted through the small room and to Chase's surprise she actually took a step toward him, her eyes glittering with anger. "She was four years old when her mother died—she needs to *know,* can't you understand that?"

"You said it yourself—Joanne is dead." He forced himself to say the words, almost relishing the pain they brought.

"And you think you've got some kind of monopoly on grief? If you weren't so damned selfish, you'd realize that there are other people in this house hurting just as much as you are. Don't you think Annie and Tom miss her? That Sarah doesn't miss her? They all need to be able to remember her, Chase. To be able to talk about her. To deal with her death together, as a family, not hide it away like something shameful."

The blood was pounding in Chase's temples and he clenched his fists. "I told you once that this was none of your damned business."

"You've never been able to let her go because you're convinced that you're responsible for her death, and you can't forgive yourself for that, can you? For being just an ordinary man. Well, listen up, McConnell—Joanne didn't die because you weren't a good enough husband. She died because sometimes good people die for no apparent reason and the rest of us just have to live with that!"

She wheeled away and snatched up her jeans and shirt and a lacy bra from the floor, then strode toward the door. "Joanne's dead," she repeated. "But your daughter's alive, Chase McConnell. Stop wallowing around in your own self-pity and start being the father she needs!"

The door banged behind her almost as loudly as it had behind Sarah, and Chase found himself, abruptly, alone. The silence seemed to crash down onto him, broken only by what might have been the sound of a child sobbing in the next room. He swallowed, feeling cold and a bit numb, and looked around at the things scattered on the floor.

Strangely, they didn't seem to hold much emotion now. He saw the faded dried corsage he'd given Joanne on their first anniversary and it made him smile; saw the blue knit sweater he'd bought her for her birthday that first year when money was so tight, and wondered why it brought so little pain. So long ago, he found himself thinking . . . it all seemed so long ago.

He swallowed again, his throat aching with a thickness that wouldn't ease, and listened to the sound of weeping. And didn't know at first if it was Sarah's, or his own.

* * *

It took Skye nearly an hour just to stop trembling. She'd listened to Chase storm out of the house with a sense of loss so strong it ached, then had wearily pulled off the sundress and got back into her own clothes. She took a few minutes to go in to Sarah, unable to do much to comfort the girl but sit with her while Sarah sobbed as though her heart were breaking. Then she went back into the spare room and started putting Joanne's things back into the carton.

She kept seeing Chase's expression when he'd stepped into this room and caught sight of her: the shocked bewilderment, the flicker of recognition, the desperate pain....

Her anger had vanished almost as soon as she'd walked out on Chase, leaving her cold and filled with a sickening sense of guilt. She should have minded her own business, she reminded herself as she struggled to shove the cardboard carton back into the closet. She should have dutifully played her wifely role, then gone home and put the whole McConnell clan out of her mind.

Except it was a little late now. A little late for everything as a matter of fact, but trying to salvage what was left of her heart. And just maybe saving Mary's Mountain, as well.

It was sheer desperation that had given her the idea in the first place. Time was running out, but she'd seen her father mobilize an entire college campus in a matter of hours in his heyday. The network was still there, still strong: people who knew people who knew still more people. Many of them were now solid parts of the establishment they'd once fought against, lawyers and accountants and businessmen, but most still had a spark of that old rebelliousness. More important, they now had powerful business contacts and knew how to work the system from the inside out.

He answered on the third ring, and Skye grinned. "Hi, Dad. It's me."

"Skye! Where the heck are you! We—wait a minute, Meadow's picking up the other phone."

"Skye!" Her mother sounded a little breathless, as though she'd just run the full length of the store. "Where are you! You scared us half to death! We've been trying to trace you down for days. Carly says you're staying on a ranch or something. She seems to think it involves a man...."

"It does. Sort of. But not in the way Carly thinks." She sighed. "It's a long story, guys. What's up? Don't tell me Granddad got arrested for growing dope in the kitchen window again."

"Skye...we, well we have something to tell you."

There was an anticipatory pause on the other end of the phone, and Skye was suddenly alert. "What are you two up to?"

"We're getting married."

Skye stood there stupidly for a moment. "Married?"

"You don't think it's a good idea?" Her mother sounded uncertain.

"I..." Skye managed a delighted laugh. "I think it's about time! When? Can I come?"

"Don't be ridiculous, Skye, of course you can *come*. I want you to be my flower girl."

"I think I'm a little old to be your flower girl. How about maid of honor?"

"We'll figure all that out later," her mother said with a laugh. "You...you don't think we're being silly or anything, do you? I mean, getting married is so...ordinary!"

"Yeah." Skye grinned broadly. "Yeah, it's wonderful!"

"I told you she'd figure it was cool," her father said.

"So, what brought on this sudden fit of social respectability? You decide that after thirty-two years it's not just an infatuation?"

"Something like that," her father said with a chuckle. "And besides, our accountant says it's better for income taxes."

Skye had to laugh. "Another victory for the establishment!"

"It's hard to be a rebel and an entrepreneur at the same time," he said good-naturedly. "So, what's up?"

"Well, I have a little problem, and I could use your help."

"Ask away."

"I'm open for suggestions, of course, but I think this is a job for the old SunShine Coalition...."

When she headed up Mary's Mountain a couple of hours later, she had no idea if he was even going to be there. Annie had given her directions, but the bay mare she was riding seemed to know where they were going with no urging. Skye relaxed into the rhythmic pace of the horse as they wound their way through stands of tall, sweet-scented firs and little meadows filled with wild flowers and the hum of bees.

The cabin sat at the edge of a meadow, with steep green-clad slopes behind it and a view of the valley and ranch far below that was breathtaking. Chase's long-legged roan gelding was grazing in a roughly fenced pasture to one side. Skye dismounted and led the mare through the gate, then unsaddled her and carried the saddle and blanket into the lean-to beside the cabin where Chase's gear was, then went to look for him.

A noisy little creek fretted its way through the meadow, its banks dotted with big poplars and clumps of birch and willow. There was a path that wandered alongside it and Skye shoved her hands into her pockets and set off to see where it led, letting the musical burble of the water and the birdsong in the trees above her ply their relaxing magic. And thinking a little idly that if Tri-Mar had their way all this would be lost.

She found Chase about a quarter of a mile downstream from the cabin, sitting on the grassy bank overlooking a deep, green pool where the stream widened and curved around an outcrop of mossy rocks. Elbows braced on his slightly upraised knees, he was resting his forehead on his braided fingers, massaging his temples with his thumbs as though trying to ease an ache. She stood in the shadows behind him for a moment or two, feeling the pain radiating out from him. Feeling the loneliness and the despair and the absolute emptiness . . . and knew, somehow, that she'd done the right thing by coming up here after him.

It took him a long while to realize she was there, even after she'd walked across to him. He lifted his head slowly and looked up at her, the surprise in his pain-filled eyes turning to gratitude, and then, a moment later, to something else. Something basic and forthright and uncomplicated, a raw male hunger that transcended past or future, right or wrong, everything but the fact that she was there and he needed her.

He reached for her, and she came, and he dropped his head against her with a soft moan as she clasped him against her. And then she slowly knelt, sliding through his grasp until she was on her knees before him.

"I need you," he whispered.

And she, smiling, simply replied, "I know."

Skye cupped his cheek in her hand and started kissing him lightly, then a moment later his mouth was on hers and she knew it was going to be all right.

He kissed her deeply, hungrily, like a man half-crazed, and his hands were fumbling with her jacket, the buttons on her shirt, the waistband on her jeans. And then, abruptly, impatiently, they were both wriggling out of denim and lace and leather, and when he reached for her again and pulled her into his arms, they were both deliciously naked.

He'd spread their clothing out as a rough blanket and as he eased her down onto it, Skye had to bite her lip to keep from crying out as his callused hands, and mouth and sly fingers discovered secrets she never even knew she had. He touched and caressed and tantalized her, kissing her breasts, her belly, her thighs and finally, to her shocked delight, the aching softness between, where he nuzzled her warmth and did things that nearly drove her out of her mind and left her weak and trembling and dazed.

There was one brief, awkward moment when Chase, suddenly remembering that she was unprotected, swore savagely and started to pull away. It was then that Skye blushed furiously and whispered something in his ear. And Chase, too bemused even to wonder where or how she'd gotten them, reached into the pocket of her denim jacket and pulled out the little package of contraceptives.

He got one out finally, his hands shaking as badly as any adolescent boy's, and when he turned to her again it was without doubt or hesitation. He was as gentle with her as he could be, suspecting that if it wasn't her first time it was close to it, but the white-hot need consuming him made it all but impossible to go as slowly as he'd have liked.

And after a while it just got away from him and he moaned something that could have been an apology and simply let go, hearing, with satisfaction, her little cries of pleasure.

It welled up and through him like an explosion of flame and he gave himself over to it totally, luxuriating in the simple awareness of being alive again, of being able to feel again. Of being able to share this kind of intimacy and closeness with a woman again. Of lying in her arms with her heart trip-hammering against his and knowing that somehow he'd come through the fire and darkness and had survived.

They lay like that for a long while, wrapped up in a tangle of legs and arms, and Chase finally rolled onto his side, carrying her with him, and smiled as she snuggled into the curves and angles of his body in that way a woman had.

It seemed—now—a little like a dream. He'd looked up and she'd been there; he'd reached for her and she'd come into his arms as though she belonged there. And then . . . then he'd been making love to her and it had been too late for doubts or hesitation, all his good intentions forgotten. Too late for anything but the magic of her body and her love, welcoming him, soothing him, healing him. . . .

"How did you know?" he murmured finally, running his hand slowly along the flare of her hip.

"Know what?" She sounded drowsy and comfortable.

"That this was going to happen."

"Didn't."

Chase gazed down at her quizzically, and she smiled, caressing his cheek with her finger. "I knew you needed me," she whispered. "That was enough."

"And . . . those?" Smiling, Chase inclined his head toward the small box lying beside them.

Skye smiled sleepily. "Those, McConnell, were simple wishful thinking."

"Mmm." He slipped his arms around her and hugged her against him, loving the feel of her, all naked and warm, her thigh drawn up intimately between his. "I like your kind of thinking, Red."

He looked down into her eyes and stroked her thick hair with his fingers, feeling a sudden aching tightness fill his throat. There were about ten thousand things he should be telling her, he thought wearily. About Joanne. About the past three years and the endless, gnawing loneliness. About the days he honestly didn't think he was going to make it and, once or twice, actually contemplated ending it once and for all.

And about how, in the past few days, he'd started feeling things he'd all but forgotten, thinking things he'd decided he'd never want to think again. About how, when he looked across a room at her and shared a quick smile, he felt alive again. About how, lying here with her in his arms, he felt the kind of hope he'd given up even dreaming of. About how he didn't want it to end. . . .

But, for some reason that had more to do with her than it did with him, he wound up saying nothing at all. She was here only by accident, after all; had been on her way to somewhere else. Maybe even someone else. And he'd already told her it was temporary. That he didn't want anything more from her than a few days of her time. It wouldn't be fair to change the rules now.

"Come on." He sat up abruptly, grinning as he scooped her up in his arms and got to his feet in one easy movement, striding toward the pool.

The creek widened at the curve, and the bottom dropped away at the far side where it met a low outcrop of rock to create a deep, still pool so crystalline you could see every ripple and fold of the sandy bottom. Chase waded out with Skye in his arms until the water was almost to his waist, then he dropped her in an unceremonious splash and dived hard and deep for the far side.

He broke the surface in a flurry of bubbles and flying water and shook his head to clear his eyes, and a moment later Skye popped to the surface right beside him, laughing and gasping for air.

Grinning, she kicked away from him leisurely, then turned and swam to the far side, where the rock wall was decked with moss and ivy and tiny white flowers. She dived again, then surfaced and swam back toward him, her hair rippling out across the water like flame, and he caught her easily. Except she slithered through his hands like a seal, laughing, and he took chase.

They played like that for a long while, laughing and splashing each other, diving for pebbles and playing tag and trying to catch the bright darting minnows that flickered through the sunlit water around them.

Finally, he reached for her lazily in the sun-warmed water and she relaxed into his arms and slipped her hands around his neck and lifted her lips to his. He kissed her leisurely, tangling his legs with hers as they kicked gently to stay afloat. He was already aroused and she moved against him unhurriedly, wrapping her legs around his thighs and teasing him with her own body, almost but never quite engulfing him.

Slipping his hands under the backs of her thighs to support her, he flexed his hips in rhythmic counterpoint, smiling against her mouth.

It was Skye who broke first, shuddering and burying her face in the curve of his shoulder with a soft moan as she tried to maneuver herself over him. But Chase held her away from him firmly, sinking his fingers into her soaking hair to tip her head back so he could kiss her again, deeply and slowly. They were at the low rocks again and he half lifted her up onto them, baring her breasts and belly, and he lowered his mouth to lick the water cascading from her. Skye moaned again and arched her back, lacing her fingers in his hair and pressing his mouth to her.

He was still in the water, floating between her parted thighs, and as he let himself slip backward, he ran his parted lips down her sleek belly, then farther down to the russet triangle at the juncture of her thighs and the delights it hid, drawing a soft moan from her even as he lifted her hips slightly and pressed his mouth to her.

She was so responsive, so willing, so trusting that it took no time at all to take her where he wanted her, and as her shuddering low cry echoed away, he pulled her off the mossy rock and into his arms and she clung to him, panting, her heart pounding against his.

"Now," she whispered, sliding her arms around his neck and drawing his mouth to hers. "Now..."

"Soon," he promised, kicking off and swimming leisurely with her to the far side of the pool, where the water shelved up to the grassy spot where they'd left their clothes. He picked her up and carried her up onto the bank, water cascading off them, then eased her down onto their makeshift bed, where he'd loved her the first time.

Her body gleamed in the leaf-dappled sunlight dancing through the canopy of green above them. And as she moved against him, slippery and wet and lithe, he groaned her name and eased himself between her thighs and then, in one slow, caressing thrust of his hips, he sheathed himself in her welcoming heat.

"I think," Chase murmured at least a hundred years later, "that we should get up to the cabin and dry us—and these clothes—off."

"I don't think," Skye murmured back, only half-joking, "that I can move."

"That bad?"

"That good."

"Hmm." He curled around to kiss her left breast, teasing the nipple with his tongue. "Straight to the ego. What man can resist?"

"If I'd had any idea—I mean *any* idea—that sex was like this, I'd have succumbed, and kept *on* succumbing, years ago."

Smiling, he sat up and scrubbed his fingers through his tangled, damp hair. "This isn't any of my business, but why were you holding out?"

"Backlash." She smiled and sat up a little unsteadily. "I grew up at the peak of the free-love generation, remember. Everyone bopping in and out of bed with everyone else. No real commitment. No. . . meaning." She grinned. "Anyway, I figured sex was vastly overrated, and decided to hold out for. . . a while." For the right man, she'd very nearly said, nearly biting her tongue in her haste to catch herself.

Chase gave a grunt, looking thoughtful, and they gathered up their wet, crumpled clothing in silence and walked back up the path to the cabin.

It was just a rough, one-room homesteader's cabin and yet it was surprisingly comfortable inside, each generation of McConnells having added its own improvements. A huge stone fireplace dominated one wall and Chase had a snapping fire going in no time and draped their damp clothing over convenient pieces of furniture.

He found a flannel hunting shirt hanging in the small closet and shook it out, then handed it to Skye with a smile. "You're a hell of a distraction wandering around like that, Red. And we only have one of these left." He held up the package of contraceptives.

"I figured three would be more than enough," she said with a slow smile.

And Chase, matching her smile with one of his own, slipped his arms around her and kissed her gently. "Three," he murmured, "is just warm-up...."

While Chase unearthed a small camp stove and made coffee, Skye laid a couple of wool blankets in front of the fireplace and sat in front of the flames, shaking out her hair to dry it. Chase joined her a few minutes later, setting two earthenware mugs of steaming coffee on the wide raised hearth and settling onto the blanket behind her.

He wrapped his arms around her and kissed the side of her throat, then pulled her back against him and rested his chin on the top of her head. "I'm sorry," he said quietly. "For this morning. For the things I said. When you found me down by the creek I'd been sitting there for hours, trying to figure out how the hell to apologize."

"Don't, Chase." Skye linked her fingers with his and relaxed against him. "I should have realized those things belonged to Joanne before I even opened the box. I had no right even looking at them, let alone..." She frowned, stroking his arm with her fingertips. "I'm sorry. For that, and for the things I said. You were right—it isn't any of my business. I have no right telling you how to live your life."

His fingers tightened around hers. "I dumped you in the middle of my problems. It's natural for you to get involved."

Involved? Skye smiled to herself. She was halfway in love with him. More than halfway....

"How's Sarah doing?"

"She's hurt and mad. I talked to her for a few minutes, but you're going to have to do some big-time apologizing to smooth things over. She doesn't understand why she's not allowed to look at her mother's things—she's at an age now where fatherly decrees don't mean much if they don't make sense."

He breathed a weary oath. "Some of what you said this morning hit pretty close to home."

His voice was rough, and his fingers had tightened around hers again. He consciously relaxed them after a moment and she could hear him take a deep breath. "I loved her," he said after a long while. "So damned much it hurt sometimes. It's been hard...letting go of that."

Skye didn't say anything, just stroking his arm with her fingers as she stared into the flames, somehow knowing that this was the first time he'd talked about it. The first time he'd been able to open himself enough to share some of the pain.

"Tup Hewitt destroyed my father," he said after another long pause, his voice cold. "Dad had overextended, buying too much stock too fast, gambling that the beef prices would go up and the transport and feed costs would come down and that it would rain when it should.

"Except we went into the first year of a four-year drought that spring, and beef prices dropped and the cost of feed to top off the calves went through the roof. We held on that first year, started going under in the second, and by the third we were all but bankrupt."

He was silent for a thoughtful moment. "He went to the bank, but they just laughed at him. I can remember watching him humiliate himself, practically begging them for an extension on the loans. Getting nothing but fat banker smiles...."

His grip on her fingers made her wince, and he relaxed it instantly. "Then Hewitt heard about the trouble we were in. He offered Dad a cutthroat loan to hold the bankers off. We had no choice—it was take his money or lose the Rocking M. The drought broke the next summer and the market picked up and little by little we started getting back on our feet. Then my father died."

"Oh, Chase..."

"They broke him—Hewitt and those damn bankers. After that, he was never the same. It's as though all the life went out of him."

"How did you meet Joanne?"

"At a stock show over in Bend. She was there with her old man, and I was selling some breeding stock and..." There was a hint of a smile in his voice. "She had every man there tripping over himself."

"And she chose you." *And what woman wouldn't?*

"Hewitt nearly had a fit. No way *his* daughter was going to marry any down-at-the-heels rancher whose sorry little spread was mortgaged to the rafters."

"But she did, anyway."

"She did, anyway. We thought...hell, we thought we were invincible. We were young and in love and nothing could go wrong." He paused. "Hewitt called me a couple of weeks after the wedding to tell me he was canceling the rest of the loan. A *wedding* present, he called it." His voice hardened. "I told him I'd see him in hell before I'd take his charity. That I'd pay back every penny, with interest, if it took me the rest of my life."

So that's where it had started: that ferocious pride, the desperate need to be independent of Hewitt money, Hewitt meddling.

"After Sarah was born, it got worse. They even flew in a specialist from Boston just to make sure Joanne had the *best* medical care possible. We practically had to build an extension to the house to fit in all the junk they bought Sarah—cradles, rocking horses, imported dolls, enough clothes to start a franchise. They even opened a college fund for her, as though I couldn't afford to educate my own daughter."

The words were hot with old resentment and anger, and Skye said nothing, just rested her head against his chest and waited until he was ready to go on.

"Hewitt wanted to buy Joanne a new car for her twenty-eight birthday. Said he didn't think it was safe having her and Sarah driving around in the old pickup." Chase's voice was tight and his fingers had flexed around hers almost painfully. "I... blew up. Hewitt and I had the worst argument we'd ever had, him accusing me of not providing for them properly, me telling him to—well, it ended with me throwing him off the ranch and telling him to never come back."

A log collapsed on the fire, sending up a tinsel-spray of sparks, and Skye watched them lift.

"Joanne and I argued about it. She wanted to take the car—said it made sense that she have it so I could have the pickup when I needed it. But I didn't see it that way. All I saw was Tup Hewitt rubbing my nose in the fact that I couldn't afford to buy it for her myself. She—" He swallowed. "She had a doctor's appointment that afternoon. I stood in the window watching her drive off and thinking maybe she was right, that when she got home I'd..."

Skye closed her eyes, not wanting to hear the rest. Wishing there were some way she could take the pain away.

"They said the brakes had gone." His voice was curiously calm, almost remote. "The driver of the truck said she was coming down that steep section of side road just where it meets the main road. He jackknifed his rig and flipped onto the median trying to avoid her, but—'' Another pause. She could hear him fighting to say the rest.

"She was pregnant. She hadn't told me yet, wanted it to be a surprise. We—we'd wanted another child.''

Skye didn't even remember turning to put her arms around him, but a moment later he was embracing her fiercely, and he groaned, shuddering as though he were fighting back the grief, the tears.

"Let her go, Chase,'' Skye whispered. "You can't blame yourself forever, you know that. Sarah needs you...'' *I need you.*

"I know...I know....''

And then, finally, it broke. A convulsive sob tore through him, a sound of utter loss coming from some deep place inside. She held him tightly, letting tears slip down her cheeks without even knowing whom she was weeping for, the laughing blond-haired woman she'd never met or the man in her arms whose pain and anguish had somehow become her own.

Another sob tore through him like something ripping loose, and she wondered, as she cradled him in the firelight and felt the wetness of his tears against her throat, how she was ever going to turn her back when this was over and walk away.

He lay on his side in the firelight, head propped in one hand, and watched her sleep. Her hair had dried into a tangle of bronze-and-copper curls and it spilled around her head in a hundred shades of red, shimmering in the light from the fire. She was smiling in her sleep, that wonderfully kissable mouth curved in that knowing little smile of a woman who's just come from her man's bed.

Or is still in it. Chase smiled and stroked her bare shoulder, loving the silk of her skin. Loving just to watch her....

And, as he had about three-dozen times in the past half hour, he found himself wondering what happened now.

They'd made love for what had seemed like hours this last time, turning to each other silently, needing no words for what they'd seen in each other's eyes. And it had been...different. More uninhibited at times, gentler at others, but there had been moments as he'd lain in her arms, body locked with hers, and had gazed down into her eyes that he'd felt something pull so tight inside him he'd thought he'd explode.

And when it was over, when they'd held each other tightly, shaken with the intensity of what had happened between them, he'd felt it again, that peculiar tenderness he'd never dreamed he'd ever feel again.

He smiled faintly and brushed a flyaway strand of hair from her cheek. Hell, if he didn't know better he'd think he was falling in love with her.

Except there was no room in a broken heart for love.

And so, again, the question: what happened now?

They weren't going to be able to pick things up where they'd left off, pretending this afternoon hadn't happened. The kind of intimacies they'd shared today *meant* something, damn it.

He should have kept his hands off her!

He sat up cross-legged, elbows braced on knees, and rubbed his lightly stubbled cheeks. He couldn't ask her to stay. It wouldn't be fair—he didn't have a damned thing to offer her. Except some pretty spectacular sex, he amended with a grin. Sexually, they were about as compatible as a man and woman can get, but even good sex can't make up for the other things.

He had a ranch that was a cat's whisker from bankrupt, with mortgages from here to eternity. A daughter who needed a couple of years' worth of mind-numbingly expensive medical care. And he himself was ... well, anything but a bargain. He still functioned on one or two levels, but he was far from the kind of man a woman like Skye deserved. She deserved love and affection and laughter and joy. She deserved everything he wished he had to give but couldn't.

If he had the sense God gave a fence post, he'd call Roy Ives and tell him to drop all the charges against her. Then he'd drive her into town, kiss her one last time and send her away. Before either of them got hurt.

Or Sarah, he reminded himself wearily. Of all of them, Sarah had the most to lose. How was he going to explain to a seven-year-old things he didn't understand himself?

He gazed down at Skye and felt that little tug around his heart again, unable to look at her enough. To touch her enough...he caught himself as he reached toward her again and clenched his fist, swearing under his breath.

Get rid of her, something whispered from a dark recess of his mind. You're asking for more trouble than you've ever dreamed of if you don't pack her the hell up and get her off this ranch....

And under it, under the sense of loss that welled up through him as he got to his feet and started dressing, under the regret that it couldn't work between them, was something that felt like raw fear.

Nine

It was the cold that awakened Skye. Chase had pulled a blanket over the two of them just before she'd fallen asleep in his arms, but the cabin was turning distinctly chilly as the sun went down. The fire had burned itself out, and she shivered as she sat up and looked around the small cabin.

It was almost dark, and she shivered again as she slipped from under the rough blanket and started to get dressed.

Chase was nowhere around. His clothing was gone, and Skye frowned as she pulled on her boots and smoothed the cuffs of her jeans down over them. Surely he wouldn't have gone back down to the ranch without wakening her.

He hadn't. He was in the corral behind the cabin, brushing down the big roan gelding. The mare stood nearby, already bridled and saddled, twitching her tail and stamping restlessly, the bit jangling as she tossed her head as though impatient to be underway.

The roan threw his head up and whickered as she opened the gate, and Chase glanced around. His gaze held hers for a heartbeat, and there was something in his eyes—a remoteness, a warning not to get too close—that sent a cool draft down Skye's spine. Her lighthearted greeting dried in her throat and she started stroking the roan's neck, pretending not to notice Chase's silence.

"Was it something I said?" She asked it as lightly as she could manage, rubbing the horse's face. He nickered softly, fumbling at her shirt cuff with soft, rubbery lips.

"It's getting late," Chase said without looking at her. He could have been talking to a complete stranger for all the emotion in his voice. "It's time we headed back."

"You should have wakened me. I could have helped."

"I can manage on my own."

"Yes." Skye watched him for a long moment, thinking that he had—inadvertently—told her everything she needed to know. *I can manage on my own.* "Yes, I know you can."

He looked around. "What do you mean by that?"

Skye managed a rough smile, pretending it didn't hurt. "You don't have to get defensive, Chase. I know today was just one of those things . . . two people, a romantic forest glade, some chemistry. It got away on us, we made love, end of story. I wasn't going to start fantasizing that it meant something and that we—" She shrugged, laughing, and reached up to wipe a smear of dust from his chin, holding his gaze evenly. "I'm a big girl, McConnell. I know the difference between sex and love. You don't have to be scared I'm going to become a problem."

He did, at least, have the decency to flush, she noticed.

He broke her gaze and turned to run the brush down the roan's long, smooth back again. "I didn't think you were, Red."

It shouldn't hurt, she told herself savagely. She'd known it didn't mean anything—he'd reached out and she'd been there, that was all. And big girls, as she'd pointed out, didn't mistake sexual chemistry for major romance. Today was a memory she'd carry with her for the rest of her life; it was a little silly to be hurt because he was being honest with her. It would be worse if he lied. Worse if he let her actually think—

She walked across to the mare and hooked the stirrup over the saddle horn so she could tighten the cinch. "This is probably as good a time as any to tell you that I want to leave. I've met your lawyer. I've met your father-in-law. I think everyone's got the message by now."

Chase straightened slowly, looking across the roan's back at her. "That wasn't the deal, Red. We said two weeks. Maybe more if there's a problem."

"You didn't say anything about *more*. You said two weeks."

"It's only been nine days."

"The deal was, I'd stay long enough to convince people we were married. I've done that. There's no need for me to stay."

Chase tossed the brush into a bucket by the fence and walked around the roan's glossy rump toward her. "Nothing's definite yet. Hewitt hasn't said anything about dropping his petition."

"Chase, enough people have seen me and talked to me to make your marriage plausible, all right? If someone asks where I am, tell them I'm...I'm visiting a sick sister." She pulled the cinch knot tight and dropped the stirrup, slapping the mare's neck.

"You didn't say anything about leaving this morning."

"We didn't talk this morning. And this afternoon we...didn't talk much, either."

"It's about this, isn't it?" He rested one arm on the mare's back and leaned on it, looking down at Skye. "About what happened this afternoon."

"You mean about spending most of the afternoon making love with you?" She looked up at him almost defiantly. "You can't even say it, can you? Fine. Then call it what it was. The word's been around for centuries." She used the street epithet deliberately, intending to shock him and managing to shock herself slightly in the process, having heard it in schoolyards and seen it spray-painted on walls often enough but never having said it herself.

Chase's mouth tightened and he caught her wrist as she reached for the saddle horn, his eyes angry. "Is that all you think today was?"

"Wasn't it?" She held his stare challengingly, daring him to deny it. Daring him to say the things she wanted him to say, things she knew he never would.

"No." His voice was hoarse and his gaze burned into hers, hot and restless and filled with something just a little dangerous.

"Sarah's going to be wondering where we are." She wrenched her wrist free and put her foot in the stirrup, then mounted before he could stop her, pulling the mare around. "I want you to sleep in the spare room tonight. You can drive me into town tomorrow."

Chase caught the mare's bridle and held her firmly, staring up at Skye. "And if I don't?"

"You will." She smiled bitterly, praying she could keep the tears back until her back was turned. "I figure you won't be able to get rid of me fast enough now, McConnell. You hate having that precious barricade of self-pity compromised—if you keep me around after what happened up here, you just might start feeling like a normal, healthy man again. And if you do that, you'll have to give up all the guilt and self-blame in the bargain.'' Skye planted her heels into the mare's ribs and the horse squealed and half reared, tearing the bridle from Chase's hand. ''And I think you like that role a little too much, Chase. I think you like the *pain* a little too much.''

''*Damn* you—'' He lunged to catch her, his face white.

But Skye had already pulled the mare around. She brought the end of the reins down over the mare's rump with a crack, and the horse leapt forward as though on springs, ears back, and headed for the fence at a pounding gallop. Half-blinded by tears, Skye didn't realize the mare intended to try to jump the fence until it was too late. Swearing with sudden fright, she leaned over the animal's sleek neck and hung on for dear life as the horse gathered her haunches and lifted into the air like Pegasus, clearing the top rail with a foot to spare. She came down on solid footing and fought for her head, and Skye gave it to her, lying low across the mare's withers and just letting her run. Knowing it could never be fast enough or far enough to outrun the ache in her heart.

When they reached the edge of the meadow and the trail narrowed and started down the mountain, Skye reined the horse into a slow trot. She was a couple of miles down the trail when she heard a horse coming up behind her at a flat-out gallop, and she steeled herself, knowing it would be suicide to try to outrun him. Even if her mare could outstrip that big gelding he rode, doubtful at best, the trail was too steep and winding to be anything but deadly to both horse and rider.

He caught up to her a minute or two later and reined the gelding in roughly beside her. The big horse reared and fought the bit, eyes rolling, but Chase held him in easily, giving Skye a hard look as he rode by her, hat pulled down low, eyes glittering slightly in the shadow of the brim.

"That was a damned stupid thing to do. Are you trying to kill yourself, or just ruin one of my best horses?"

To Skye's relief he didn't even wait for an answer, just rode by her to take up the lead. She wiped her eyes with her sleeve, hoping he hadn't seen the tears, and tried to tell herself that it was better this way. That she'd never hoped for anything else.

They rode the rest of the way at a hard, fast canter and both horses were lathered and hot by the time they reached the corral. Tom watched them ride in, his face hardening as he looked at the horses, hardening even more when he looked at Chase's expression.

"You okay, honey?" he asked gently as he helped Skye dismount.

"I'm fine," Skye lied, managing a rough smile.

"I'll rub these two down." Tom took the gelding's reins from Chase. "You'd better get up to the house. Annie's holding dinner, and the child's worried you've rode yourself over a cliff. And you've got company."

"Who?" Chase growled.

Tom just looked at him. "I guess you'll find out soon enough."

Chase swore and strode by the other man, his face hard, and Skye bit back an angry comment. It was, she decided as she followed him toward the house, going to be a cheery little evening.

"Well, if it ain't about time you two showed up!" Annie glowered at them as they came into the kitchen, looking hot and out of sorts. "Sarah's been half out of her mind all afternoon, thinking Skye'd run off without saying goodbye and that *you*—" she fastened a hostile look on Chase "—had stormed off and had an accident."

"Sorry," Skye murmured, unable to hold Annie's angry stare. "We—I . . . lost track of time."

"Got a good sunburn on you." Annie cocked her eyebrows. "Looks like it goes all the way down, too. You weren't up there skinny-dipping at the pool by the old cabin, were you?"

To Skye's annoyance, she felt herself blush, and Annie gave a snort. "Quite a love bite on your neck, too." She gave Chase a speculative—and not entirely unpleased—look. "So there's a little life in the old horse, after all, is there?"

"Put a lid on it, Annie," Chase growled, striding across to the doorway.

"Don't you sass me, mister," Annie shot right back. "You might be more or less growed up, but you still mind your manners in this house or you'll answer for it!"

He muttered something that could have been an apology, and Annie flashed Skye a broad grin. "Had yourself quite an afternoon, did you?"

Skye's cheeks were still hot, and she tried to slip past the older woman, unable to meet her amused gaze. "We…ummm…he showed me the old homestead, that's all."

"I just bet he did," Annie said with a salacious chuckle. "That boy never was no slouch when it came to the ladies, and I don't figure being out of the saddle for three years hurt him much. In fact, I figure after three years, he—"

"Annie, please!"

"I just hope you're being careful. I'll drive us into town tomorrow and take you in to the pharmacist. He'll fix you up with—"

"I'm leaving tomorrow," Skye said calmly. "So I don't—"

"Well, there you are!" The brisk female voice coming from behind her made Skye wheel around. The tall, beautifully dressed woman standing in the door to the dining room smiled as she made her way across the kitchen, high heels clicking purposefully on the hardwood floor. She held a ring-bedecked hand toward Skye, her eyes cool and just a little amused.

"I'm Sarah's grandmother, Barbara Hewitt. And you've got to be Chase's new wife."

She was one of those women who had always intimidated Skye, beautiful and exquisitely turned out and completely self-assured. Everything about her was expensive and perfect: her hair, the designer-label slacks and coordinating sweater, the subdued makeup. The type of woman who could wear diamonds and heavy gold in abundance, yet not look out of place in a casual ranch kitchen, she radiated old money, good schools and a comfortable certainty of her place in the world.

The type of woman, Skye thought with a sinking heart, who could make a formidable opponent if you got on her wrong side.

"Mrs Hewitt!" Somehow she managed to collect her wits and take the proffered hand, smiling with feigned delight. "I'm so sorry I wasn't here—you should have let us know you were coming!"

Barbara's smile said more clearly than words that her unheralded arrival had been planned that way. Although what she'd hoped to catch them at, heaven alone knows, Skye thought a little irritably.

"Chase was showing me around Mary's Mountain and we lost track of time. I hope you haven't been waiting long."

"Oh, Sarah and I put the time to good use, catching up on our visiting," Barbara said with a smile. "She certainly sings your praises, my dear. You've made quite a hit with her."

"She's made quite a hit with me, too," Skye said with a smile, trying to ignore the other woman's assessing gaze. Her hair—hard to control at the best of times—had dried into a completely unmanageable mass of tangled curls, and her shirt and jeans were wrinkled and still had bits of dried grass clinging to them. Between that and the all-too-obvious love bite on her throat, she figured it had to be pretty obvious what she and Chase had been doing all afternoon. "Are you going to be able to stay for supper?"

Barbara smiled gently at her. "Actually, I'm staying for a few days. If it's convenient, of course."

"Oh..." Skye felt her heart turn over. "Of course," she managed to get out, her mouth aching with the effort to keep smiling. "We're delighted to have you. I've heard so much about you from... from Chase and Sarah and... everyone."

To her surprise, Barbara gave a quiet laugh. "You're a liar, my dear, but I appreciate the courtesy. Tup was quite taken with you, and I think I can see why. I'm looking forward to having the opportunity to know you better."

"Yes." Skye wondered if she was half as pale as she felt. "Yes, that will be... wonderful."

"I heard you say something about leaving when I came in...? I hope I didn't catch you at a bad time."

It was the kind of innocent question that made the back of Skye's neck prickle, and she found herself wondering just what Barbara knew...or thought she knew. How long had she been standing at the kitchen door listening? Just what had Sarah told her? What had Tup Hewitt said that had brought her out here so promptly?

Chase caught Barbara Hewitt's question just as he stepped into the kitchen, and swore he felt his heart stop. Skye was standing near the counter looking decidedly rattled, and as her gaze lifted and met his squarely and they stared at each other across the width of the kitchen, he held his breath. She could end it right here, he thought numbly. One or two words, and it would be over. And in a way, maybe it served him right....

"Nowhere important," she said quietly, eyes locked with his. Then, abruptly, she broke his gaze and looked at Barbara with a warm, open smile that seemed to fill the kitchen. "I was just thinking about going down to Portland to do some shopping, but there was nothing that can't wait. Have you taken your things up to one of the guest rooms yet? I think the big blue one up at the end is the best—it's got the nicest view."

And Chase felt such a surge of pure affection for her in that moment that he could have walked across and kissed her, good intentions be damned.

"Skye! You're back!" Sarah appeared at the door just then, eyes wide and small face registering relief. "Oh, I'd thought you'd—"

"I'm sorry, honey!" Laughing, Skye dropped to her knees and gave her a huge hug. "I didn't mean to be so long." She smoothed Sarah's hair back and gazed at her seriously. "Are you all right?"

Sarah nodded. She leaned down and whispered something in Skye's ear and Skye smiled and gave her another hug, which was returned so enthusiastically that Skye groaned in protest. "Okay, off you go to wash your face and hands."

"Hey, peanut," Chase said cautiously.

"Hey yourself." Sarah rubbed at an imaginary spot on the front of her T-shirt.

Chase winced and hunkered down on one heel, shoving his hat back with his thumb. "I...uh...guess you're still pretty sore at me, huh."

"No." She said it a little too casually, still not looking at him.

"I'm sorry I yelled at you this morning, Sarah," he said quietly. "I wasn't mad at you, I was mad at . . . hell, at the world, I guess. And I'm sorry I took it out on you. It wasn't fair."

"I'm sorry for going in there to play when you told me I wasn't s'posed to," she whispered. "Hug?"

"Hug!" He swept her up in a fierce embrace that made her squeak. "Love you, peanut."

"Love *you*, Daddy," she whispered.

"Can we be friends again?"

She nodded, breaking into a sweet smile that made his heart turn clear over. Then, sparing Skye another love-filled grin, she hobbled through the door and down the corridor to the bathroom.

Chase eased himself to his feet. Slowly, drawing in a deep breath, he turned to face Barbara Hewitt...and found himself face to face with Skye instead.

Smiling, she slipped her arm around him. "Darling, would you take Mrs. Hewitt's bags up? Then we'd both better get cleaned up for supper—I'm sure everyone's starved, and it's all our fault."

Her smile was warm, almost cheerful, but there was a flicker of warning deep in her eyes, a hint of concern that he might do something reckless.

"I love you," Chase murmured, bending down to brush his lips against hers, and for that heartbeat of time he meant it. Cradling her against him, he looked across at Barbara and extended his hand, swallowing his hostility. "It's good to see you again, Mrs. Hewitt."

Barbara clasped his hand and gave him a dry smile. "This new marriage of yours must be having a mellowing influence. There was a time not too long ago when you'd have told me to get out."

"I've said a lot of things in my life that I've lived to regret," Chase said with only a hint of irony.

To his surprise she just nodded, her expression curiously wistful. "I suspect we all have, Chase," she said very quietly. "I just wish..." She caught the thought and smiled, shaking her head to dismiss it. "I think I'll get freshened up before supper, too."

"Supper'll be on the table in fifteen minutes," Annie said from behind them. "So don't *none* of you take too long on this freshening-up business."

Chase, still holding Skye in the curve of his arm, let Barbara Hewitt walk through the door ahead of him. Then almost regretfully, liking the way she felt against him, he dropped his arm from around Skye and followed her out of the kitchen, trying to ignore the way the soft denim of her jeans hugged her bottom. And the vivid image he had of making love to her not a handful of hours ago, her sitting astride him, back arched, dark-tipped breasts taut, the muscles in her flat stomach flexing as she lifted and moved all around him, engulfing him....

His body responded so urgently that it made his breath catch and he gritted his teeth as he walked up the stairs behind her, wondering how in heaven's name he was going to get through the next few days without losing what was left of his mind. And trying not even to think about what it would be like to simply follow her into the bedroom and ease her out of her shirt and jeans and under things and stretch out on the big bed with her and spend the next hour or two buried so deep inside her they'd breathe as one....

As the bedroom door closed behind them, Skye let her shoulders sag and scooped her hair back from her face with both hands, eyes closed. She should have blurted out the truth right there in the kitchen, she thought wearily. Should have gotten it over with once and for all instead of making things even worse by lying through her teeth, playing that ridiculous charade of smiling, sweet wife.

She'd *sworn* it was over. She'd had every intention of leaving in the morning, regardless of the kind of opposition Chase put up. And then Barbara Hewitt had walked through that door and Sarah had come in and a moment later Chase had appeared . . . and in the next breath she'd heard herself stepping back into the role as though she'd been born into it.

"Thank you."

Chase's voice was just a murmur by her right ear, and before she could move, he'd settled both hands on her shoulders and had kissed the side of her throat where she'd pulled her hair back.

"I owe you for that, Skye."

"Yes," she said with precision, stepping away from him very carefully, "you do."

"You're going to stay."

"Don't think I'm doing this for you," she said with hostility, striding across and sitting on the bed with a flounce. Not looking at him, she struggled to pull her boots off. "I'm doing it for Sarah. Because as much as I detest *you* at this moment, I can't convince myself it would be in her best interests to live with the Hewitts."

"For what it's worth, I'm sorry about what happened out there today."

"So am I." She flung one boot across the room and fought to get the other one off, telling herself ferociously that she was *not* going to cry. Not in front of him.

"I don't mean making love with you," he said quietly. "I'm not sorry about *that* one damned little bit. I mean what happened afterward. Walking out on you like that. I..." He swore softly and started pacing restlessly. "It all happened so fast! Hell, Red, I'm so mixed up I don't know whether I'm coming or going...."

"And you think I do?" The other boot came off abruptly and she flung it after the first, needing to throw *something*. She got to her feet and started rummaging through the closet for her dinner dress. "I didn't anticipate this any more than you did, McConnell. And I just want to forget it, all right? I'm going to write the whole day off as an indiscretion and I don't want even to think about it again." Which was a lie. There wasn't going to be a day during the next fifty years that she wouldn't remember this afternoon. And Chase.

"That suits me just fine, lady," he growled, throwing himself into a chair and pulling his own boots off. He was frowning thunderously, his face dark with anger and resentment and a dozen other things. "I don't need any damned complications in my life. I've got more complications than I can handle right now!"

They both reached the bathroom door at the same instant and stood there glaring at each other. Then Chase motioned her to go ahead and stalked across to the closet to dig out a clean shirt, wincing as the bathroom door banged behind him. He tossed the shirt across the bed and stripped down to his briefs, swearing under his breath as he realized he couldn't even shave until she was through...damn it, it *was* just like being married!

Except if he were married, he reminded himself irritably, he'd join her in the shower and maybe, with luck, wouldn't get around to shaving at all!

Swearing again, he strode across and gave the bathroom door a sharp rap, then pushed it open without waiting for a reply. Opening the cabinet, he took out his razor and a can of shaving foam, then wiped the misty mirror clear with his arm, trying to ignore the indistinct but unmistakably naked female form moving around behind the glass doors of the tub enclosure. It took no effort to remember what she'd felt like in his hands, wet from the pool, her skin sleek and slippery and—

"Damn!" He winced, swearing as a dab of blood swelled up from the nick on his jaw.

There was an inhalation from behind the glass doors, then one of them slid back cautiously and Skye's dripping head poked out. "What are you doing in here!"

"Shaving," he replied very reasonably, staunching the cut with a bit of tissue.

"But you can't just come in here when I'm—"

"There's nothing you have I don't already know by heart," he drawled, meeting her angry gaze in the streaky mirror.

Her eyes widened, then her dripping head vanished and the sliding glass door banged shut. The shower went off after a few more minutes, and the door again slid open a scant inch or two. "Would you at least hand me a towel?" she asked in a subdued voice.

Chase took one from the rack by his elbow and shoved it at her. "How long do you suppose she's going to stay?"

"Mrs. Hewitt?" There was a thoughtful pause, punctuated by the unsettling sound of a towel being rubbed over naked, wet flesh. "A day or two, maybe. You don't..." The tub door slid open and Skye stepped out, chastely wrapped in the big towel, her wet hair heaped on top of her head. She was frowning. "You don't suppose she's planning on staying longer, do you?"

Chase rinsed his razor under the tap, then continued to shave. "Damned if I know. I can't figure out why she's here at all." He gave the razor a shake and put it back in the cabinet, then turned to face her, wiping the rest of the foam from his cheeks with a towel. "And I want to thank you for what you're doing. There aren't many women who'd go through with it, especially after today. I know you probably hate my guts, but I swear I'll make it up to you somehow. After I get the money from Tri-Mar for Mary's Mountain, I'll—"

"I don't want your money, McConnell," she said with surprising gentleness. "The only payment I want is knowing that Sarah is healthy and walking again."

There seemed to be something else he should be saying to her, Chase thought. Something beyond the carefully polite phrases and the awkward small talk; something about that afternoon, and what it had been like lying naked with her in the dappled sunlight and holding her and making love to her. Something about the tightness in his chest when he thought of her leaving, and the ache he knew was going to fill his long and empty nights.

He found himself reaching for her without even thinking about it, his fingers skidding on the wet skin of her arms and shoulders, and for half an instant he found himself not giving a damn that he'd sworn not to touch her again. Not even caring that if he made love to her this time it would be unprotected . . . fantasizing for that heartbeat of time of having her pregnant with his child, of marrying her, of raising a family with her, of—

Her lips were actually under his before he managed to come to his senses and he wrenched his mouth from hers and turned away. Not even looking around, he stripped off his briefs and stepped into the tub.

It took nearly ten minutes of cold water to get himself cooled off enough even to think about getting dressed and going down to supper. Wrapping a towel around his hips, he walked back into the bedroom, prepared for the worst.

His tan slacks were lying on the bed, along with the clean shirt he'd pulled out, briefs and socks, a narrow leather belt and his good tooled-leather boots. But Skye was nowhere to be seen, just a lingering trail of some musky, erotic perfume hanging in the air to tell she'd been there at all.

And Chase, frowning thoughtfully as he started to dress, found himself thinking that for a man who'd sworn he didn't want any complications in his life, he seemed to be going out of his way to prove himself a liar.

He was still kicking himself as he made his way downstairs, half-convinced that he was going to find that Skye had made good on her threat to leave.

Instead he found her in the living room with Barbara Hewitt, the two of them laughing merrily over something like long-lost friends, drinking what looked like white wine from two crystal glasses he'd forgotten he even owned.

Skye had braided her long, thick hair into two flat plaits and had wrapped them around her head like a coronet, securing them with a couple of fancy combs. Loose tendrils curled around her face and neck and she looked like a medieval princess out of one of Sarah's fairy-tale books. Her dress was a simple knee-length emerald green knit affair that managed to show off every inch of her lithe body and slender legs without even trying hard, and it took Chase a moment or two to get his breath back.

"You're gaping at her like a boy going to his first prom," Barbara said dryly. "You'd think you'd never seen her dressed up before, Chase. How long did you say you've been married?"

"I...haven't. Seen her in this dress before, I mean." Smiling, he kissed the side of Skye's throat, letting his mouth linger on her scented skin. "What are you trying to do to me?"

"Pretending to be the perfect little wife," she whispered sweetly. Aloud she asked, "Wine, darling?"

"I didn't think Chase drank white wine," Barbara said from behind him.

He had his mouth open to say something dismissive when Skye looked up at him as though in surprise. "You don't?" When he cautiously shook his head, she just laughed. "Well, that's what you get when you marry a man you haven't known for long—one surprise after another!"

"Just how *did* the two of you meet?" Barbara Hewitt strolled across to stand by the fireplace, her eyes a little too speculative for Chase's taste. "I'm sure it must have been quite romantic."

"In—"

"—jail," Skye completed, smiling up at Chase. "Isn't that right, darling?"

"More or less," he said warily.

"Really?" Barbara's eyebrow lifted. "That sounds fascinating."

"Actually, it wasn't quite *in* jail," Skye corrected. "I was in the police station on . . . business, and Chase came in to talk with Roy Ives, and things sort of went on from there."

"Ives? You mean here in town?" Barbara's voice sharpened. "But I didn't think you were from around here, Skye."

"I'm not." Skye cast Chase a cool look. "But half an hour after meeting Chase, I was . . . captivated."

"And you've been married . . . how long?"

"Not quite two weeks," Chase said evenly.

"Two weeks! Good heavens, you're still on your honeymoon."

Skye's gaze met his almost by accident just then and Chase was amused to see a blush spread delicately across her cheeks. She looked away swiftly, taking a sip of her wine, and for a moment he felt himself almost wishing that it were true.

Supper wasn't as difficult as he'd imagined it would be. Skye, to his everlasting gratitude, put her hostility aside and impersonated a loving wife and gracious hostess so perfectly that even he found himself believing the illusion a couple of times.

He kept having to remind himself that she was just playacting, that the loving upswept glances she cast his way were fake, that the way she'd let her fingers linger on his hand or arm was part of the role.

And after the meal, when they'd gone into the living room with coffee and Skye had settled on the sofa beside him, nestled into the curve of his arm and body, he had a strange sense of disorientation, as though Joanne had been the fantasy and this laughing, redheaded woman the reality.

He was still thinking about this when he took Sarah upstairs to bed. As he tucked the sheet around her and kissed her good-night, she smiled up at him sleepily. "She's sure nice, isn't she?"

"Your grandmother Hewitt?"

"Skye! You like her a lot, too, don't you?"

"Yeah, I like her okay," he replied casually.

"Why don't you marry her for real so she can live with us?"

Chase looked at her warily. "What do you mean?"

"I know you're just pretending," Sarah said patiently. "Did Skye tell you that?"

"Nope. I just knew."

Chase swore to himself, rubbing his eyes. "Sarah, it wasn't—"

"Oh, I know why you're doing it," she went on blithely. "It's okay. I didn't say anything to Grandma Hewitt. I just told her I was really glad you'd married Skye."

Terrific, Chase thought wearily. Now he was teaching his daughter to lie. "Look, peanut, we—"

"So, are you going to marry her for real, or what?"

"I was married to your mother, Sarah," he said quietly. "I don't want to be married again."

"Why not?" She gazed up at him curiously. "Didn't you like being married to Mom?"

"Yeah, I liked it," he whispered. "I liked it a lot. That's why... Sarah, it's too complicated to go into tonight, all right?"

"But if you *liked* being married to Mom, and if you really *like* Skye, I don't see why—"

"Sarah!" He scrubbed his fingers through his hair, not having an answer that satisfied even himself.

"Will you *ever* get married again?"

"Maybe one day. Look, would you go to sleep? It's late."

"I'd like another mother someday," she said very softly, her voice wistful. "One like Skye ..."

Chase's stomach gave a flip-flop and he rubbed his face wearily, not liking the ideas Sarah was putting into his head one little bit. "Maybe someday," he muttered, reaching across to turn off the lamp. "Now go to sleep, peanut."

He was halfway to the door, when her sleepy voice stopped him. "She likes you, you know. I think a lot." Again he felt his stomach give that odd little twist. "I bet if you just asked her, she'd stay."

No, she wouldn't, peanut, he told her silently. It's all just pretend. Just make-believe and fairy dust....

It was after eleven by the time Skye finally got to bed. Too keyed up with tension and sheer exhaustion to sleep, she lay in the darkness of the big bedroom and tried to convince herself that everything was going to be all right. That the cool speculation in Barbara Hewitt's eyes didn't mean anything, that the pointed questions about her, about the marriage, were just normal curiosity. That the woman was just here to visit her son-in-law and his new wife and her young granddaughter, not to find the weak spot in their story and come in for the kill.

How in God's name was she going to get through much more of this? It was exhausting just trying to keep one step ahead of the woman, thinking every answer through before opening her mouth, trying to anticipate the next question, the possible implications of every word she said, looking for the trap....

Restless, she rolled onto her back, turning her head to look at the clock. After midnight. And Chase still hadn't come back.

Maybe he wasn't going to. He'd been on edge and quiet all evening, and as she and Barbara had come up to bed, he'd gone outside, muttering something about checking the stock. Skye glanced at the comforter and pillow that she'd placed on the floor for him, frowning.

Perhaps, like her, he was uncomfortable with the idea of sharing a room with her after what had happened that afternoon and was sleeping somewhere else tonight. Which, although easier on both of them, probably wasn't very smart, considering Barbara Hewitt was just down the hall and would no doubt wonder why the new groom was sleeping in the stable instead of with his wife.

She was still thinking about this nearly half an hour later when she heard the kitchen door open downstairs, then the measured tread of boots on the stairs. The bedroom door opened softly, closed again, and she could hear him moving around cautiously in the dark, swearing under his breath as he bumped into a chair.

"It's all right," she said quietly. "I'm not asleep."

"Sorry. Did I wake you?"

"No." She raised up on her elbow and reached across to turn on the bedside lamp, squinting slightly against the glare.

"I went riding for a while. It helps me think."

"About Barbara Hewitt?"

"About you." He gave her a speculative glance from the other side of the room. "About us."

She didn't say anything. He was wandering restlessly, looking troubled and uneasy, and Skye felt her stomach knot very slightly.

He looked across at her for a long moment, his expression guarded, then walked across and took something out of his jeans pocket and tossed it onto the bedside table, his grin a little reckless, a little rueful. "I found these in the bunkhouse."

Skye looked at the package of contraceptives, feeling a little chilled, and wondering what he expected her to say. "You're a romantic devil," she finally whispered, hoping he couldn't hear the hurt in her voice. "Is this the cowboy version of courtship, McConnell? Or do you just figure that after today it's a forgone conclusion?"

"Neither." He sat on the edge of the bed heavily and rested his elbows on his knees, pulling his hat off and rubbing his face wearily with one hand. "I've spent the past hour trying to figure out how to ask you to marry me," he said very quietly. "I was going to ask you to marry me, then I was going to make love to you. With you. And in the morning I was going to drive us into town and find a justice of the peace, and make it legal."

For a fraction of a second, Skye felt as though she'd stepped off a moving train. She blinked stupidly at him, wondering if she was going to wake up any time soon now. He was staring at the floor, turning his hat in his hands, his profile a little hard in the lamplight.

"There have probably been more romantic proposals in the history of the world," she said just as quietly, wondering how she could be so calm. "I presume your use of the past tense means you changed your mind somewhere between the bunkhouse and here."

"I know it's crazy, but Sarah gave me the idea." He turned his head to look at her, his eyes holding hers. "She needs you, Skye."

And you? she asked him silently. Do you need me, Chase McConnell? And even if you did, could you ever bring yourself to admit it?

"It wouldn't be forever or anything," he added after a moment, looking troubled again. He resumed his contemplation of the rug between his feet. "I figure a year max. This whole thing with the Hewitts will blow over in a few months, and the worst of Sarah's surgery will be behind her by next summer. We can get a quiet divorce, and that'll be the end of it. I'd make it worth your while, of course...."

"Of course." He made it sound so simple, she thought. So simple it almost made sense—if you didn't think about it too closely. She deliberately toyed with the idea, taunting herself with it....

"Anyway, I don't expect you to tell me your answer right away or anything. I know it's a hell of a decision— you've got your job to think about, things like that." He glanced at her again, looking serious. And tired, Skye thought. So very tired. "I know you don't owe me the time of day, but you seem fond of Sarah. And I was just hoping..." He shrugged.

"I don't know what to say." She lay back and stared at the ceiling, feeling a little numbed. Knowing she couldn't possibly agree to such an insane scheme. And yet, way down deep, wondering why not. Wondering who could be hurt if she did say yes.

"Don't say anything." His voice was hoarse. "Just think about it, all right?" He looked at her again, and he reached out suddenly and smoothed a tangle of hair off her shoulder. "I don't have a damned thing to offer you but my word I'd never hurt you, Skye. It might not be your perfect made-in-heaven marriage, but it wouldn't be the worst one around, either."

And in that moment Skye very nearly felt her willpower give away. She thought of the little girl sleeping just down the hallway, of the laughter and love and happiness in this house, of lying in Chase's arms only a few hours ago and feeling the kind of joy she'd only dreamed of. All she had to do was say yes.

"I'll think about it," she finally said, already knowing what her answer had to be but wanting, even for a little while, to pretend it was possible. She reached up and ran her fingers down his cheek, marveling at the male strength in the hard contours of his face, in the rasp of stubble against her hand, in the aura of power and control he radiated, even at rest. "In the meantime, why don't you turn out the light and come to bed."

He smiled faintly and turned his face to kiss her cupped palm, nodding toward the comforter and pillow lying on the floor. "I appreciate your letting me bunk down in here again. I'd sleep in one of the other rooms like you wanted, except with Barbara here..."

Skye held his gaze steadily. "That's not what I meant, Chase."

Ten

Something changed around his eyes, a slight tightening perhaps, a wariness, as though he half expected some kind of trap. "Does this mean you—"

"It doesn't mean anything, Chase." She put her fingers lightly across his lips. "It's just what it is."

He didn't say anything. Then something shifted almost imperceptibly in his expression, something predatory and hungry, and Skye felt a delicious little shock of anticipation shiver through her.

Straightening, he tossed his hat onto the dresser, then bent down to pull off his boots. He set them aside with deliberation and then, not taking his eyes from hers, he eased himself to his feet and started unbuttoning his shirt.

It was the most erotic thing in the world, lying there watching him undress, knowing he was coming to her. He took his time, pulling his shirt off and tossing it aside, then unhurriedly reaching down to unbuckle his leather belt, pulling it free of the loops and dropping it at his feet. He smiled a little as he unbuttoned the waistband of his slacks and drew the zipper down, his eyes smoldering with memories of that afternoon, and Skye shivered again.

And then he was naked, his body lean and golden in the lamplight, and he was reaching for the sheet, tossing it aside, and in the next moment he'd eased himself into her waiting arms.

The bed gave a faint squeak of protest at their combined weight and they froze, staring at each other, and in the next instant were both convulsed with laughter.

"Shh," Skye managed to get out between giggles. "Barbara's just down the hall!"

"I'd forgotten all about that damned squeak," Chase murmured. "The only time you ever hear it is when...this happens."

"This?" Grinning, Skye wrapped her arms around his neck.

"This," Chase whispered as he lowered his mouth to hers.

And then he was kissing her in that deep, slow way he had that made her melt right to her toes, and Skye just let herself relax into the heat pulsating through her. Not giving a damn about how right or wrong it was, about whether she'd stay or go, about any of it...just knowing that this, for a little while at least, was what she wanted. This, at least, she could have.

He eased her out of her baby-doll pajamas and spent a long and delicious while teaching her more about herself than she'd ever imagined possible, and an even more delicious while teaching her about him and all the erotic possibilities of a man and a woman who are in no hurry at all. And when he finally settled between her thighs and took possession of her with one strong downward thrust of his hips, she was so achingly ready for him that she had to press her hand to her lips to keep from crying out.

They made love gently and slowly, wanting quiet and privacy in a house seemingly filled with people, trying not to give the treacherous bed any reason to advertise what they were doing. Chase moved very slowly, the flex of his hips strong and yet tightly controlled, and Skye slipped deeper and deeper into a haze of pure physical pleasure, his lovemaking all the more erotic for its restraint.

And at the end, when release finally came, he dropped his mouth over hers to stifle her soft cry of satisfaction. They relaxed into each other's arms, hearts pounding in unison, and as Skye nestled against him, she found herself idly wondering if perhaps this wouldn't be enough, after all... :

The next two days were a blur to Skye. All she remembered, really, was smiling. That, and the growing feeling of panic. But it was the constant smiling that was the hardest, trying to be upbeat and pleasant and so damned *nice* it hurt.

Not that Barbara Hewitt wasn't just as nice. But there was an edge to her smiles that had Skye constantly on guard, a cool watchfulness that had her so self-conscious that just walking across a room made her feel guilty.

It was only the nights that made it bearable—the long nights with Chase, making love halfway to dawn and then waking in his arms to make love again. Those idyllic hours with him seemed a time apart, stolen from the worry and the concern and the constant lies and make-believe.

And yet at times she felt torn apart, playing one role to Barbara Hewitt during the day and another to Chase at night—trying to reassure the one that she loved him, and the other that she didn't.

She was contemplating the irony of this late on the third afternoon of Barbara Hewitt's visit, hiding out in the bedroom with a feigned headache while Sarah took her grandmother down to the pond to visit Hamlet.

Too restless to lie down, she'd finally brought in the ironing board and a big basket of clean laundry and was attacking a pile of Chase's cotton shirts, discovering that wielding Annie's heavy old steam iron for an hour or so worked off one heck of a lot of tension and frustration.

She had put the finishing touches on a blue denim workshirt and was reaching for a hanger just as a brisk knock sounded at the door. It swung open and Barbara Hewitt smiled coolly at her.

"May I come in?"

"Of course." Skye's heart sank, but she plastered a pleasant smile across her mouth and finished hanging up the shirt.

Barbara strolled across the room, looking fresh and cool. "That's almost a lost art in this day and age of drip-dry." She watched Skye shake out another shirt and lay it across the board. "I always found it a relaxing pastime."

"Yes, it is."

Barbara glanced around the room. "It seems strange, being in here and knowing Joanne's gone. Seeing you here, instead."

Skye stiffened very slightly, concentrating on straightening the shirtsleeve. "It must be difficult for you."

"I have to admit that when I first heard that Chase had remarried, I was...well, I was infuriated. It seemed unfair that he should be happy when my daughter is—" She bit it off. "A day or two later I stopped feeling sorry for myself and started feeling pleased for Chase. These past three years haven't been easy on him, either."

Skye looked around, wondering what was coming. "And now?"

"Now?" Barbara gave a soft laugh. "Now, my dear, I think it's time we stopped playing games." She looked across the room at Skye calmly. "You're not really married to my son-in-law, are you?"

Even braced for it, Skye felt her heart skip a beat. But she didn't say anything, hoping against hope that it was just a bluff. That Barbara was just shaking the bushes to see what fell out.

"This whole thing is an elaborate sham to make my husband and me believe he's providing Sarah with a stable home." She smiled. "It was easy enough to check. I simply went down to the Department of Records and intimidated the clerk until she confirmed what I already suspected." She shook her elegant head. "I can't imagine how Chase thought he'd get away with it. Or how on earth he talked a bright young woman like you into playing along with it. If I didn't know better, I'd suspect the man was blackmailing you."

In spite of herself, Skye had to smile. "Closer than you realize, but it's a long story. Does Mr. Hewitt know?"

"Not yet." Barbara resumed her slow stroll around the room. "He doesn't trust Chase, but he believed you. You're *very* good."

"Not good enough, obviously."

"Only because I know Chase a little too well. I'll admit that even *he* had me fooled a couple of times, but marrying a woman out of the blue like that . . . no. It didn't fit."

"So." Skye turned the iron off and carefully set it aside, then looked across at the older woman who had, in the space of a few words, become an opponent. "Now what?"

"I imagine the lawyers Tup has investigating this entire situation would find it an interesting scenario."

"By the time you told them," Skye said very calmly, "Chase and I *would* be married. Legally married."

Barbara looked at her for a quizzical moment. "You'd actually do that? Marry a man you don't love to make a point?"

"Not to make a point. To keep this family together. Sarah belongs here—with her father."

But Barbara was still gazing at her, eyes a little too shrewd. "No, I'm wrong—you do love him, don't you?"

It would be pointless to deny it, Skye decided. She simply shrugged, not saying anything.

"And Chase? How does he feel?"

"Chase is still in love with Joanne."

"Chase *thinks* he is," Barbara said quietly. Thoughtfully. "He feels he should be. But I've seen how he looks at you." She frowned suddenly, shoving her hands in the pockets of her slacks and turning to look out the window. "This will undoubtedly sound strange, but it's time Chase let go of Joanne. She's dead. It's taken me a long while to come to terms with that myself—or as much as a mother ever does when her child dies. But I've learned that if you're going to survive emotionally, you've got to release them."

She turned to look at Skye. "Chase is still torn apart with guilt. It's not his fault the brakes on that old truck went out, but he's still beating himself up over it. Not, God knows, that Tup's been any help. But Chase deserves to be happy, Skye. For Sarah's sake, as well as his own."

Skye found herself struggling to make sense out of what she was hearing.

"We—Tup and I, I mean—did everything wrong with those two." Barbara smiled reminiscently. "Neither of us thought Chase was the right man for Joanne. She was our one and only and we...oh, we told ourselves that we wanted the best for her, but of course it was just fear. Fear that she'd leave us and that would be the end of her. It was especially hard for poor Tup—he saw Chase as some sort of rival for Joanne's love."

Skye didn't say anything, sensing Barbara needed to talk this through without interruption. "I came to terms before Tup did with the fact that Joanne loved Chase. The truth is, I've always admired Chase. He's a strong man, an honorable one. One of the few men I've ever seen stand up to Tup Hewitt and win. And he loved Joanne—there was no denying that."

She frowned slightly, looking out the window again. "It was hard for them, of course, with so little money. We . . . like so many parents, we couldn't keep from meddling! We offered Chase money to help him out." She shook her head. "Now, of course, I can see it was the worst thing we could have done. A man has to believe that he's capable of supporting his own wife and family. We thought we were helping, *thought* we were doing the right thing by our daughter. But what we were doing was antagonizing Chase so badly we nearly lost both of them."

She turned to look at Skye. "Chase thinks we tried to lure Joanne away from him with money and gifts, but actually we were just fighting desperately not to lose her. And that's why Tup is fighting so hard now—the same fear. Fear that Chase will take Sarah away and we'll never see her again."

"And Chase is fighting like a cornered cougar because he thinks you're trying to take her away from *him.*"

"I know." She sounded weary and passed her hand across her eyes. Then she looked up at Skye again, smiling wanly. "I love my husband, but he's not the easiest man to live with. He's stubborn and proud and would rather walk on nails than admit he's wrong."

Skye had to smile. "A little like Chase."

"Exactly like Chase. Why do you think they've been at each other's throats for so many years? Tup sees in Chase the son he never had, and he forgets that Chase is very much his own man."

"It seems a shame," Skye said carefully, "that two men with so much in common can't find some way to solve their problems."

Barbara's gaze held hers. "I've often thought that myself."

"Chase won't give Sarah up, I think you know that. He'll sell the Rocking M right down to the planks in the floor if he has to, but one way or another, he *will* keep her."

"And Tup, of course, is just as determined that we should have her." She shook her head impatiently. "It makes me heartsick to think of Chase having to sell Mary's Mountain to meet Sarah's medical bills. Especially when Tup and I have more money than any two people need." She paused delicately. "If we could just convince Chase and Tup to see it that way."

"There . . . might be a way."

"They'd accuse us of conspiring against them, of course."

"Of course." Skye had to smile. "I called my father about this situation with Tri-Mar a few days ago, and asked him what he could come up with in terms of a counter offer."

"Your father's in real estate?"

She looked so surprised that Skye had to laugh. "You might say that. He and my mother own an organic greenhouse and garden plot." Then she sobered. "Dad knows everyone worth knowing in the environmental movement, and he got hold of a group calling itself World First.

They're buying up bits and pieces of land all over the west coast and turning them into wildlife preserves, protecting the natural habitat against poachers and development and so on."

"Does Mary's Mountain fill the requirements?"

"Perfectly. It's never been cleared or under cultivation so is original wilderness. The cabin and family cemetery could stay, and Chase would have free access to the land. In fact, World First would require it, to discourage hunting or poaching."

"My God!" Barbara's face glowed. "And Chase would still get the money he needs for Sarah's medical care?"

"Yes."

"What's the catch?"

"World First needs more money to match Tri-Mar's bid."

"How much more?"

Skye took a deep breath. "About a half million."

Barbara didn't even blink. "And Chase won't know the money came from us? If he finds out, he'll sell to Tri-Mar just to spite Tup."

"World First gets a lot of anonymous private donations."

Barbara's eyes had a definite twinkle. "I won't be able to tell Tup what he's donating the money for, of course. If he knew it was going to help Chase keep Sarah, he'd have a fit."

Skye winced. "You don't think we're being a little... sneaky?"

Barbara looked mildly indignant. "Of course we're not being sneaky. It's just a matter of not confusing them with too many facts. Men don't deal well with a lot of facts, I've found. Give them too much information and they feel obligated to complicate even the simplest little thing." She smiled conspiratorially. "Just think of it as being resourceful. Men like resourceful women."

"And this...?" Skye's gesture took in the entire house. "What are you going to tell your husband about Chase and me?"

"Nothing." Barbara's mouth curved in a smile. "I came down here to see for myself what kind of a home Chase was making for Sarah, and I'm quite happy with what I've seen. I intend to tell Tup that. And I can assure you that Sarah *will* be staying with her father."

Skye nodded, feeling her cheeks taking on an uncomfortable warmth. "I owe you an apology. I've done nothing but lie to you since we've met."

"Well, I'll agree that you haven't been as honest as I'd like, but I have to admit that I admire the hell out of you!" She laughed. "I like a woman with strong convictions. And with the courage to go with them. Any young woman who'd put herself on the line to fight for a man and his child as you've done over the past few days deserves respect."

Skye smiled faintly. "I think you're being charitable, but thanks."

"What are you going to do about Chase?"

"What do you mean?"

Barbara smiled and walked toward the door. "It took me a long while to admit this, but my daughter was a remarkably lucky young woman to have found Chase McConnell. Any woman would be. He's worth fighting for, Skye." She paused at the door and looked around. "And my granddaughter needs a mother."

"But I don't *want* you to leave!" Sarah clung to Skye's neck, sobbing. "It's not fair! Dad was supposed to ask you to stay!"

"He did." Skye was finding it hard to fight her own tears as she hugged Sarah fiercely. "And if there was any way I could stay, I would, Sarah, I swear that. But I have to go back."

"Seems to me," Annie said gruffly from the other side of the kitchen, "that if the young Lord were to ask you proper, you'd have plenty to stay for."

Only the entire world, Skye thought. Gazing down into Sarah's tear-filled eyes, she forced herself to smile. "You take care of Annie, your dad and *yourself,* all right?"

"And you promise you'll come and visit me when I'm in the hospital in May?"

"I'll be camped out on the lawn, waiting." Skye bent down and kissed Sarah's damp cheek one last time. "Love you, Sarah."

"Love *you,*" Sarah sobbed. "Hug?"

"Hug." Skye clung to the little girl for a long while, eyes stinging with tears, then she gave her another quick kiss and released her, standing up and collecting her handbag.

Annie was by the door, looking uncharacteristically subdued, and Skye tried to smile at her. "You take care of yourself and Tom," she managed to whisper.

Annie just nodded, then swept Skye into a rib-bending embrace. "I'm sorry it didn't work out, honey. For him, as much as you. You're going to find yourself some nice young man, but he...well, he's going to miss you for a long, long time. Almost as bad as he missed Joanne, I think."

"I've got to go. Tom's waiting." Blinking her eyes clear, Skye managed a rough smile. "Let me know when Sarah's next operation is scheduled—you've got my address."

"I'll take care of it, honey, don't you worry. You take care of *yourself* down there in the big city. And don't…well, don't spend a lot of time thinking about him, all right? You get on with your life and be happy. You can't do nothing for a man that doesn't *want* to be loved."

"'Bye, Annie." One more hug, a kiss on the cheek, and she was free. Out the door and into the sunshine, trying to tell herself it was exactly what she wanted…freedom to go back to her own life again, to put the entire two-week incident at the Rocking M out of her mind.

And if she believed that, Skye thought grimly as she walked across to where Tom was waiting by the pickup truck, she was a far better liar than she'd ever given herself credit for. The best she could hope for was to make a pretense at living her life until the worst of the pain had gone, and then, maybe in a thousand years or so when her heart had healed, she'd be able to think of this place without crying.

Eyes swimming with tears, she didn't even see Chase standing by the gate until he reached out and took her small suitcase from her hand.

"I'd hoped you'd change your mind." His voice was rough. "I told you last night we could work up some sort of contract. I could pay you for helping Sarah with her schoolwork and—"

"I have a life to go back to, Chase. We agreed on two weeks, remember?"

"I remember." His eyes glittered. "But that was before, damn it."

"Before?" Say it, Skye willed him. Just *say* it!

"Before we…got close."

"Before we started sleeping together, you mean."

A muscle ticked along the side of Chase's strong jaw. "You make it sound as though it doesn't mean anything."

"It doesn't," she lied, forcing herself to hold his angry stare. "Men and women sleep together all the time, Chase, and it isn't anything more than what it is. We knew that, remember?"

"I told you I'd marry you."

"It's not enough, Chase," Skye said wearily. Wanting more than anything just to leave, now, before she said something stupid.

"What the hell do you want, then!" He shoved his hat back and glowered down at her, perplexed and angry.

Everything you can't give me, she felt like shouting at him.

"Sarah needs you, damn it!" He struggled with it for a moment, his face darkening. "And I... I need you, too." The words sounded torn out of him.

"I know you do." Smiling, she reached up and touched his cheek, wondering how she was ever going to close her eyes without seeing his strong, hard-edged features in her mind, or go to sleep without dreaming of eyes the color of storm clouds. "But you don't love me, Chase."

He stared down at her, something shifting deep in his eyes. Pain. Regret. Maybe just wishful thinking.

"I can't fight a memory. If it were another woman, I'd fight for you with everything I have. But I can't compete with a dead woman. Until you can let her go, there's no room for anyone else. And I—" She had to swallow hard, "I love you, Chase McConnell. But I won't settle for *need.* I won't settle for being a substitute, just filling up a cold, empty spot in your bed. I want *all* of you, or I don't want any at all."

"Skye—" His face was white and he reached for her.

"No." Carefully she stepped away. "Don't, Chase— please. If you say anything else I'm going to cry...." She managed a sob of laughter, her eyes filling even as she said it. "These two weeks with you have been the closest thing to magic I've ever had, and I'll treasure them all my life. But we both know it has to end. I *do* love you...."

And with that, she fled.

"Look out! Behind you, McConnell—look *out!*"

Chase glanced around in time to see the stallion coming at him like a juggernaut, ears peeled back, neck stretched out. Squealing with rage, the horse reared, flailing out with both front hooves.

One caught Chase on the shoulder and smashed him against the rail fence, knocking the wind out of him, and he swore breathlessly and ducked as those deadly iron-shod hooves flickered by his head. Diving to one side, he hit the ground and rolled under the bottom rail of the fence just as the stallion's hooves pounded into the soft dirt where his head had been a second before.

"You okay?" Tom Lindquist and two of the hired hands came tearing over, and Tom reached down to help Chase to his feet. "That horse doesn't appear to like you much, son."

"The feeling's mutual," Chase growled, giving the stallion a hostile glare. He took his hat from the young fellow who'd picked it up and slapped it against his jeans, raising a cloud of dust. Wincing, he examined his torn shirt. The flesh under it was scraped and oozing blood, already swelling and starting to discolor. "For two cents, I'd sell him here and now."

"Couple of those young mares we brought in yesterday are in season and his blood's on the boil, that's all," Tom said gently. "Like any healthy young man when his mind's on a woman, he doesn't take well to feeling a rope on him."

Chase gave a snort, wincing again as he shrugged his shoulder experimentally. Everything seemed to work, but it was going to be as stiff as hell in the morning.

"We could use a couple of more hands when we start bringing the stock down." Tom tipped his hat onto the back of his head and wiped his sweat-runneled forehead with his arm. "Got a good calf crop this year. With beef prices where they are, you'll do all right. Get a good start on paying those loans back."

"Yeah, it's starting to come together finally." Chase put one foot on the lower rail and crossed his arms on the fence, watching the young stallion as he snorted and pawed restlessly, neck and tail arched, every inch of him vibrating with sexual energy.

The mares were in a corral nearly a quarter of a mile away, but the wind must have been carrying their scent and the stallion squealed again and kicked at the fence, throwing his head and half rearing. "We're going to have to put a logging chain on him to keep him in here tonight," he muttered. "He's going to bust down every fence between here and those mares if we're not careful."

"Maybe he's got the right idea. He knows what he wants and he goes after it. Nothing complicated about horses."

"If you've got something to say, say it," Chase grated. "You've been on my case all week."

"I've been keeping an eye out for you, if that's what you mean. You can't seem to keep your mind on anything lately. This young stud would have taken your head clean off if I hadn't been here. Just like yesterday when you got between that cow and her calf—she'd have got you if I hadn't been there to rope her." He shook his graying head, skewering Chase with an impatient look. "You're an accident looking to happen, son. You're going to have to put her out of your mind once and for all and attend to busi-

ness, or go after her like you should have three weeks ago
and stop acting like a horse's—"

"Go into town this afternoon and see if you can hire a
couple more hands." Chase settled his hat down over his
windblown hair and turned away. "The money from
World First should be coming in any day now. The bank
said they'd carry us until it does."

"Damn it, McConnell, you're hurting so bad you can't
even think straight. Swallow your pride and go after that
girl before some other young fella grabs her and you lose
her for good! Because I'll tell you, you're never going to
find another one like her."

Not bothering to answer, Chase headed for the house to
change his shirt and get his shoulder cleaned up. They were
going to be too damned busy over the next couple of weeks
with roundup and branding for him to risk being laid up
with an infected shoulder. Tom was right—they had a hell
of a good calf crop this year. Between that and the sale of
Mary's Mountain...

He swore wearily, tired of even making the effort to
pretend he cared. Truth was, he didn't give a damn about
any of it. He'd been going through the motions for weeks,
hoping that sooner or later the misery would lift and he'd
start to feel something again. He glanced toward the picnic tables in the backyard as he walked through the gate,
cursing himself as he did so.

She wasn't there. Hadn't *been* there for damned near a
month now. Yet still, he found himself looking. Hoping
that maybe—

Maybe what, he asked himself brutally. That she'd
changed her mind about marrying him and had come
back? That she'd decided need was enough after all...?

It wasn't. Need could capture a woman, but it wouldn't
hold her. Even if she did come back it would only be for a

little while, just until she realized it wasn't enough and left again. And he couldn't take losing her a second time.

"Dad! Daddy, guess what! Hamlet's got another Ophelia!"

"What?" Forcing the other thoughts from his mind, Chase grinned at Sarah as she burst through the back door, her eyes sparkling with excitement. "You mean she made it back, after all?"

"No, it's another one! Hamlet's found *another* one." Her eyes suddenly widened. "What did you do to your shoulder?"

"I went a couple of rounds with that young stallion we brought in yesterday," he said carelessly, tousling Sarah's hair as he walked into the kitchen. "How about getting the antiseptic from the bathroom and playing doc?"

"My Lord," Annie said digustedly when she saw him. "You don't stop letting your mind wander, Chase McConnell, you're going to make that poor child an orphan!"

"My mind did not wander," Chase said between his teeth. "I've been knocked around worse than this. Comes with the job."

Annie gave a snort. "It's true, you know. Old Hamlet came back last night with a new wife."

"Good for Hamlet."

"Seems to me that it's a sorry state when a bird's got more sense than a grown man."

And Chase, pouring himself a cup of scalding hot coffee, found himself thinking that it was going to be another long, hard day.

But a few hours later, sitting on a sun-bleached log at the edge of the pond down in the lower meadow, he wondered if maybe—just maybe—Annie hadn't been on to something.

The tall reeds to either side were filled with red-winged blackbirds and about a million frogs, and the air was heavy with the tang of slough water. A flotilla of swans glided by, as elegant as figurines on a mantel, and an untidy flock of ducks swooped in and around and down, landing with ungainly splashes.

And to one side, ignoring it all, Hamlet swam in leisurely circles around his new bride, preening and chuckling, looking as fatuous as any groom on his honeymoon.

"So you really did it, you old reprobate," Chase said softly, watching the big bird as he lifted his wings and spread them, raising and lowering his head as he danced for his lady.

He'd beaten the odds, Chase mused. Most old ganders his age wouldn't even bother if they lost their mate, following the ancient genetic code that dictated they live the rest of their lives alone, part of a flock but never part of that closer family bond.

He looked happy, Chase thought. Happy and content. As though he'd said his goodbyes to the lost Ophelia, done his grieving and had moved on to the next part of his life with joy and a renewed love of life.

Idly Chase let the memory of Joanne's laughing face drift into his mind, bracing himself for the pain.

Except it didn't come. What he felt instead was a curious sense of release: sweet, almost wistful, not loss as much as something to be treasured.

And with it, another feeling. Deeper. More intense. More certain.

"You're right, Hamlet," he muttered suddenly, getting to his feet. "Damn it, I think you're right...."

He hit the door to the kitchen at a flat-out run, startling Annie so badly she dropped a spoon and it went clattering across the floor. Sarah was sitting at the big table, reading one of the books Skye had left her, and Chase grinned broadly as he tossed his hat onto the chair beside her. "Stay right there, princess. Don't you move."

"What?" Sarah stared at him. "Where are you going?"

"Upstairs. I'll be back in a minute."

He took the stairs two at a time, and hauled the big box out of the back of the closet in the spare room and pulled it open. The photographs were in three big envelopes and he tucked them under one arm and dug around for one of the empty albums he knew should be under all the other things.

Sarah was still sitting at the table when he came down, looking a little alarmed, and Annie eyed him warily. "You feelin' okay? That horse didn't crack your head this afternoon, did he?"

"I'm just fine, Annie." Smiling at Sarah, he pulled one of the chairs out and sat down, then spilled the contents of the first envelope across the table. "Sarah, I think it's time I told you about your mother. And while I'm doing that, we can start putting these photos in the album."

Her eyes widened, filled with uncertainty at first and then, as she started to realize he was serious, with barely suppressed excitement.

"Annie?" He glanced over his shoulder at the older woman, seeing a gentleness in her eyes that hadn't been there for a long while. And what could have been the glitter of sudden tears. "How about forgetting those dishes for a while and coming over here to help me with this? I don't know half the people in these pictures. And you can help me tell Sarah all about Joanne—hell, you two had secrets I still don't know about."

Annie came over and sat down, giving her cheek a surreptitious swipe with the corner of her apron. "Well, it's about time."

"I want to clear all those boxes of Joanne's things out of the attic," Chase said quietly. "Go through them with Sarah—keep anything she wants or that you think she should have, then get rid of the rest. If you find anything you think the Hewitts might like, keep that out, too. I figure they'd like some of these snapshots."

"I figure there'll be a few things in those boxes you might like yourself," Annie said softly.

Chase nodded, smiling. "Yeah, I suspect there is. I'll go through them myself when I get back."

"Back?" Sarah looked up. "Back from where?"

"Portland. I have something to do down there."

Annie smiled triumphantly. "I hope this *something* stands about five foot high and has hair the color of dynamite."

"Skye?" Sarah's eyes widened with excitement. "You're going down to see Skye?"

"I'm going to try," Chase told her quietly, frowning a little. If she'd see *him,* he thought with an inward wince.

"Well," Annie said flatly, reaching for a handful of the photographs, "all's I can say is, you'd better not come back here without her. Not if you know what's good for you."

Epilogue

Chase stood leaning in the open door of the cabin and stared out across the sweep of star-filled sky. It arched above and around him, confettied with a million twinkling stars, and he wondered if his great-grandfather had stood in this same spot and had looked at that sky and had decided that this was where he was going to build his home.

That first McConnell had come out here with nothing but a wagon, two strong hands and a dream. And his young wife. His beloved Mary. They'd lived under canvas for most of the first summer while they had built this cabin, and from that start they'd sent out strong roots. Five generations's worth, Chase thought with a smile. From the patriarch, Brian McConnell himself, to young Sarah, sound asleep down at the ranch at the moment.

He looked around at the woman lying asleep on the bed behind him, red hair spilling around her head, lips curved in a smile. Just looking at her made his stomach tighten with anticipation and love, and he shrugged away from the door and padded across the rough-hewn floor, still naked, and slipped under the sheet and blankets.

Skye stirred and opened her eyes sleepily. "Hi."

"Hello, Mrs. McConnell." Smiling—and feeling inordinately proud of himself—Chase slipped his arms around his new bride and tugged her in close to him. "Damn, you're good to come home to!"

"How long have you been away?"

"About five minutes," he said with a husky chuckle. "About four and a half too long...."

Slipping her arms around him, Skye cradled her head on his shoulder and sighed with contentment. "I wonder if Annie will come up here tomorrow morning with our wedding breakfast."

"I wouldn't be surprised." Chase kissed her cheek. "She thought we were crazy, spending our wedding night up here."

"Personally, I thought it was the most romantic thing I'd ever heard." Skye lowered her mouth to kiss his chest. "Although the whole day has been strange in a way. I kept having to remind myself that it's real this time. Poor Roy Ives looked a little befuddled, and I'm not too sure Phil Duggan really believes it, either. Talk about déjà vu."

"It's real," Chase murmured, lacing his fingers with hers and holding her left hand out so he could gaze—again—at the wide gold band gracing her third finger.

"I wonder if Hamlet found that piece of wedding cake we left him."

"I'm sure he did." Chase grinned and kissed her again. "You scared the hell out of a couple of the wedding guests this afternoon, lighting out for the pond in your satin shoes with your gown and veil flying behind you."

"Well, I just figured he and 'Phelia deserved some celebratory cake in honor of the part *they* played in all this."

"I guess that means you aren't having any second thoughts or anything."

"What do you think?" Smiling, she brushed his lips with hers.

"I think one of these days you're going to have to tell me how the World First people managed to swing that deal to buy Mary's Mountain right out from under the Tri-Mar's nose."

She shrugged delicately. "I told you. I called Dad, and Dad called some friends and one thing sort of led to another and—"

Chase kissed her, shutting her up. "I mean the *real* story. You and Barbara Hewitt looked like two cats who'd just swallowed the same canary today."

Skye looked up at him with wide, innocent eyes. "What do you mean?"

Chase gave a snort of laughter. "I don't know, that's what scares me. Tup Hewitt came over to ask me if *I* knew what was going on. We both figure we've been roped and tied, but can't quite figure out how."

"You worry too much," Skye murmured against his mouth. "The only thing that should be on your mind is how much I love you...."

As it always did when he heard the words, Chase felt his heart do a slow cartwheel. He smoothed her hair back from her face with both hands and gazed down into her eyes, unable to get enough of her. Of the reality of what they'd become. Man and wife. The words still gave him goose bumps.

"And I love you, Skye," he said very softly. "I still need you...God, I'll go on needing you until the day I die. But I *love* you." He kissed her gently, just letting his lips rest on hers. "I never thought I'd be able to say that again. Never thought I'd ever feel this way again...."

"Show me," she whispered, touching him with gentle, coaxing hands. "Show me again..."

And Chase, drawing her gently over him, started to do just that. Her eyes were heavy lidded and she caught her lower lip between her teeth and gave a stifled moan as he lifted his hips gently, cleaving flesh with flesh. "I love you," he whispered, reaching up and tugging her gently down into his arms. And for half a moment, gazing at the love reflected in her eyes, he could have sworn he felt the very mountain smile.

*   *   *   *   *

Harlequin Romance ®

Delightful

Affectionate

Romantic

Emotional

Tender

Original

Daring

Riveting

Enchanting

Adventurous

Moving

Harlequin Romance—the
series that has it all!

HROM-G

HARLEQUIN PRESENTS

HARLEQUIN PRESENTS
men you won't be able to resist falling in love with...

HARLEQUIN PRESENTS
women who have feelings just like your own...

HARLEQUIN PRESENTS
powerful passion in exotic international settings...

HARLEQUIN PRESENTS
intense, dramatic stories that will keep you turning
to the very last page...

HARLEQUIN PRESENTS
The world's bestselling romance series!

Harlequin® Historical

If you're a serious fan of historical romance, then you're in luck!

Harlequin Historicals brings you stories by bestselling authors, rising new stars and talented first-timers.

Ruth Langan & Theresa Michaels
Mary McBride & Cheryl St. John
Margaret Moore & Merline Lovelace
Julie Tetel & Nina Beaumont
Susan Amarillas & Ana Seymour
Deborah Simmons & Linda Castle
Cassandra Austin & Emily French
Miranda Jarrett & Suzanne Barclay
DeLoras Scott & Laurie Grant…

You'll never run out of favorites.

Harlequin Historicals…they're too good to miss!

HH-GEN

HARLEQUIN®

I N T R I G U E®

THAT'S INTRIGUE—DYNAMIC ROMANCE AT ITS BEST!

Harlequin Intrigue is now bringing you more—more men and mystery, more desire and danger. If you've been looking for thrilling tales of contemporary passion and sensuous love stories with taut, edge-of-the-seat suspense—then you'll *love* Harlequin Intrigue!

Every month, you'll meet four new heroes who are guaranteed to make your spine tingle and your pulse pound. With them you'll enter into the exciting world of Harlequin Intrigue—where your life is on the line and so is your heart!

Harlequin Intrigue—we'll leave you breathless!

INT-GEN

David Niven
and
Priscilla Rollo

In 1939, David Niven became the first British actor in Hollywood to volunteer for active service and return to England to rejoin the army. It seemed the proper thing to do: he was a descendant of two generations of professional soldiers. In fact, his father was killed at the Dardanelles during the First World War, when David was five years old. David's father would have been proud. His son distinguished himself as a commando and attained the rank of colonel. Niven married Priscilla Rollo, the daughter of an officer in the Royal Air Force, in 1940. They had two sons, and sadly, Priscilla died from injuries sustained in a fall in 1946. Niven had just completed filming *The Curse of the Pink Panther* when he died at the age of 73 in 1983. The final dialogue had not yet been looped in and Canadian impressionist Rich Little had to be brought in to dub Niven's voice. Aside from a legacy of fine films, he left his fans two witty autobiographies, both republished under the title, *Niven*.